HIS
HANDS

HIS
HANDS

A story of renewed hope
by Yvonne Lehman

To Lisa, John, Cindy, and Simon,
who accompanied me on a research trip
of white-water rafting, excursion train rides,
accommodation adventures, and great eating,
and to my readers and editors for their
invaluable input.

Special acknowledgment to Craig Plocica
of Nantahala Outdoor Center for his expert
information on white-water rafting down the
Nantahala River, and to Watchman Nee for the
analogy of "rails of a train being like prayer."

Your faith is far more precious to God
than mere gold. So if your faith remains strong
after being tried by fiery trials, it will bring you
much praise and glory and honor.
(1 PETER 1:7)

PROLOGUE

Since it had happened before in the local paper, Matthew MacEwen expected making headlines again would be accomplished as an artist, not as a statistic of Flight 323 on which he'd departed from Atlanta that morning.

Ping.

The soft sound and lighted signs, "Fasten Seat Belts Please," halted the conversation between Matthew MacEwen and his friend Bruce, who had the aisle seat.

Matthew's strong, twenty-two-year-old, beautifully formed hands curved over the armrests. He looked out the window while the pilot welcomed the 296 passengers to New York City—the Big Apple. He'd already felt the landing gear release. The flight couldn't have been more perfect on such a clear mid-June day. The pilot reported, "The afternoon ground temperature is a mild 81 degrees."

Matthew smiled at the sight of New York and the East River glistening in the sunlight. He'd like to paint this scene. Watching the big city rising to meet them, he braced himself for the exhilaration to come—not from the speed of landing, but from the prospect of what lay ahead of him.

"This is the first day of the rest of your life" had sounded like a trite phrase to him—until today.

The sound of success resonated in his being.

The sound—

A shot? A bomb?

Matthew's head jerked around. His eyes met the blank stare of his buddy. A breathless moment of silence prevailed like it did in a football stadium before a field goal is kicked.

Then the ball is flying through the air.

The onlooker feels suspended.

Will there be the shout of triumph?

Or the groan of tragedy?

It loses momentum.

It begins to drop.

It falls.

The explosion of the crowd is deafening.

It's no longer a playing field. Life is not a game.

Screaming, wailing, pleading humanity was entombed in a red-blue ocean of flame rushing past the windows. They'd burn to death.

I don't want to die.

Metal ripped. The wall of fire fell, along with the wing, creating a gaping hole. The ground rushed to meet them.

God help!

Matthew bent over and clasped his hands together at the back of his neck. Was that what the flight attendant had instructed in case of an emergency? He hadn't really listened.

Sliding. Scraping. Swaying. Maybe that would slow them.

He felt as if his seat were being torn out from beneath him. But he was still in it. The belt held. He opened his eyes. He wasn't dead. The plane leaned on the side with the gaping hole.

A flash drew his attention. Above them, the remaining engine had burst into flame.

Putrid fumes assaulted his nose and throat. Bruce unbuckled his seat belt. Matthew did the same.

Automatic response shoved him to his feet.

Outside, sirens wailed.

Inside, people wailed.

Whimpers. Crying. Praying. Shouting.

He stared. The scene looked like a giant had stepped

on a toy plane, smashing it to smithereens. But this wasn't a toy. This was real. He mustn't think about it.

He saw gaping mouths and still-staring eyes filled with horror and disbelief.

"Fire!"

A fire burned at the back of the plane.

Smoke poured from the first-class section.

Passengers coughed, yelled. "Get out. It'll blow."

A man helped a woman who limped on one foot.

Most people lay lifeless in their seats.

Some hung over into the aisles.

Hurt people cried for help.

Others ran, shoved, pushed to get to an exit.

A couple of men pounded and screamed at the bent emergency exit. Finally it gave way.

"That one's alive," a man shouted. "Help me."

Another man turned back. They struggled, but the woman's legs were trapped.

Bruce pulled on Matthew's arm. "Let's get out of here."

Matthew followed Bruce as burning fuel created intense heat.

They reached the gaping hole. Seats had been torn away completely. They must have gone down with the wing.

Smoke came up from under the plane, obscuring visibility at the escape hole.

Bruce jumped out.

Matthew heard a moan from first class.

Bruce called for Matthew to jump, even if he couldn't see. He could hardly breathe. Primal instinct said, "Jump!"

He heard the moan again. A pitiful cry for help.

Matthew ran into first class. The door of the cockpit hung open. Seats were burning. The odor was horrific. He'd never smelled burning flesh before. The air hung thick with smoke.

Overhead bins hung open, some precariously dangling. Luggage lay in the aisle and covered lifeless people.

A girl with blood soaking her hair and oozing down her face was bent over trying to unbuckle the seat belt of the woman across from her. An open suitcase lay on the seat beside the girl. A piece of metal, like the corner of a picture frame, was sticking out of her back.

Fire caught on the clothes scattered on seats behind her.

"Come on," he urged.

She moaned. "My parents."

"I'll come back for them."

Matthew knew he was lying. The woman lay with her head on a man's shoulder as if resting, but her head hung too low to be natural. The man's open mouth and staring eyes said it all.

Matthew ran toward the girl. The fire reached her before he did.

Her hair flamed. He swatted at it. It wouldn't stop burning.

She screamed. Whether from the fire in her hair or his pulling her into the aisle, he didn't know. Maybe both.

He needed a breath of fresh air but dared not breathe deeply. If they didn't get out soon, the smoke inhalation would kill them both.

She slumped to the floor. He knelt beside her, able to get a breath of the thick smoky air. He put out the flames in her hair with his hands, but the back of her dress caught fire.

He started to pull out the piece of metal. Then an old movie registered in his mind. A guy had been shot with an arrow. It mustn't be pulled out or he'd bleed to death. Matthew slapped out the fire as best he could around the metal in her back. Her flesh was burning. He smelled it. He felt it. The burning cloth stuck to his fingers.

He dragged her farther down the aisle, fearing he would pass out from lack of oxygen. The smoke was thicker, the fire closer. He picked her up, trying to be careful of the piece of metal. He followed the sound of distant voices.

Forever seemed to have passed. Apparently, it hadn't. He couldn't see. He couldn't breathe. Somehow he escaped through the hole, still holding the girl.

Someone grasped his arm and hurried him away

from the plane. He caught a whiff of clean air and filled his lungs like a swimmer coming up at the last moment for a breath. The girl lay limp in his arms.

"I'll take her," someone said.

"Don't lay her on her back," Matthew cautioned.

The person took her from him and lay her on her stomach. He spoke with sorrow in his voice, "This one didn't make it."

"She has to," Matthew said. "Get help for her."

"There're not enough ambulances here yet," the person said, hastening away. "We have to take the ones we can help first." He hurried to someone else, calling, "We need a stretcher over here."

Matthew lifted his hands in a futile gesture.

What was this?

Slowly, realization struck. His hands had no skin on them. They were red and raw, skinless, oozing with fluid.

Burned.

They began to throb. Ache. Pain like he'd never felt seared his fingers. He'd touched a hot stove when he was a child. He'd had a blister. That pain was magnified a thousand-fold. He almost focused on an attendant. "I need help."

"Others need us worse right now. Sit down, and we'll get to you."

Sit?

Dazed, he lowered himself, without the use of his hands, and sat hard on the tarmac. He bent his knees and braced his forearms on them.

Right before he lost consciousness, he stared at his future, his hopes, his dreams, his talent stretched out in front of him—burned, blistered, aching.

And for what?

He'd saved only a piece of picture frame.

The girl was dead.

ONE

Seven years later. . .

Upon arrival at the Asheville, North Carolina, airport, Christine Norwood acquired a map of the area and rented a car.

Once off the interstate and onto the two-lane roads, she feared she might drive into a mountainside. She soon realized she could snake right through the lush foliage that hugged the pavement and rose to great heights, often forming a canopy shutting out the bright evening sunlight. Beginning to trust her ability to take the curves, she relaxed.

A service-station attendant had assured her she was headed in the right direction. After six o'clock, she saw a sign. "Nantahala White-water Rafting Ahead."

Soon, she spied the "Nantahala Center" sign in front of a big building made of weathered, dark gray boards. She pulled into the gravel parking lot and exited the car.

The sound of rushing water drew her gaze to the river behind the center and several other rustic buildings. Off to the right in a reserved section stood big blue buses with rafts and canoes fastened to the tops, and "Outdoor Adventures" printed on the sides.

A building on her left displayed a "Slow Joe's" sign. Casually dressed people were eating on its two-level deck, some of it covered, some open. Men, women, and children sat outside at picnic tables in the shade of huge trees between the building and the river.

Christine headed toward the center, wondering if Matthew MacEwen would be inside. Did he work this late or would she have to wait longer? She'd already waited for seven years.

Determined, she took a deep breath and walked up the steps onto a plank porch beneath an overhanging roof and surrounded by a wooden railing. She opened the screen door and stepped into a room, its contents momentarily obscured. The smell was dank, and the air humid.

"Could I help you, young lady?"

Her eyes began to adjust to the change in light, and she walked across the worn hardwood floor, aware of dark-paneled walls and a countertop opposite her. She stepped up to the partition. "Hi," she said to the elderly man, who wore a friendly smile. "Does a Matthew MacEwen work here?"

"Work?" He laughed. His bright blue eyes squinted, and the skin at the corners of them wrinkled. "Let's say he comes around occasionally." He peered as if looking for signs of appreciation for his remark.

Christine obliged him with a smile. "Is he here today?"

With a jerk of his thumb over his shoulder, he said, "He's on the river. Should be back in. . .oh, an hour or so—maybe two."

Two hours! Christine wondered how she could survive her escalating emotions for two hours. "How will I know him?"

"Just keep your eye on that dog tied to a tree. Matthew won't leave without her." He laughed. "Or without that blue pickup of his."

Christine walked outside and stared at the long-haired golden retriever lying in the shade. She knelt beside the dog fastened to a chain around a big oak. A ceramic bowl held dry dog food.

The dog sniffed at her outstretched hand, then stood, stretched, wagged its tail, and whined. Its big brown eyes seemed to plead, "Take me away from here."

Christine petted the dog and promised, "I'll be watching you."

For two hours?

A growl from her stomach reminded her she hadn't eaten dinner. After purchasing a taco salad and diet drink from Slow Joe's, Christine sat at a small picnic table beneath a tree with roots above the ground and long limbs stretching toward the water. She didn't bother to close her eyes while thanking God for the food. Her thoughts had been a constant prayer since embarking on this journey to find her rescuer.

While sitting in the shade, enjoying the cool, moist breeze, Christine realized that the primary sound was not traffic but of sparkling water rushing over rocks in the shallow section of the river a few feet from her. People talked amiably; birds ventured close to the tables, seeking crumbs. Squirrels skittered along a path leading off into a more wooded section.

Christine thought of the California beaches that she loved. The sound of the surf could lull one into dreamland.

This setting awakened her. She felt alive and aware of nature, the rushing river, the animals, and the forest. She thought it a beautiful haven protected from the hurry-scurry of the rest of the world.

The beach looked like the top of the world as the vast ocean blended into the horizon. Here, the setting reminded her of being at the bottom of a huge forested volcano surrounded by mountain peaks rising into the sky. However, California was at sea level while these mountains stood high above it.

Things were not always what they seemed.

This situation wasn't what she had dreamed of either. For years she'd wanted to find her rescuer and thank him. Her grandparents had been against it until after she graduated from college. She'd known a young man had saved her life. In her search, she'd found out the names of three young men who had survived the crash.

She'd located Randall Jones in Minnesota. He didn't know who saved her.

She hadn't been able to reach Matthew MacEwen.

She had written to Bruce Canton, an artist with a New York book publishing company. She related her reason for contacting survivors of the plane crash. If he was not her rescuer, she'd asked, could he provide any information?

She reached into her bag and pulled out his reply that she'd read many times.

Dear Miss Norwood,

I'm so grateful that you survived the crash. I'm not the one who saved your life. That would be my friend Matthew MacEwen. I'm sorry to say that I haven't kept in touch with him over the years. I understand your wanting to find him and thank him face-to-face.

I think you need to know that Matthew's hands were terribly burned. The last time I saw him, he was very bitter. He was twenty-two then and already acclaimed as having extraordinary artistic talent. An artist's life is in his hands. I'm not trying to make you feel badly. I'm trying to warn you that he may not be receptive to your seeing him.

However, a visit from you may be exactly what he needs. He thought you died.

Please forgive me if I've been too blunt.

I don't know where Matthew is now. While in college I went with him to Nantahala in the mountains of western North Carolina where his grandpa had a white-water rafting company. I saw his grandpa again when Matthew was in the hospital.

Matthew had an aunt and uncle here in New York. We planned to live with them while in art school. Right after the crash, they moved back to Scotland.

After reading your letter, I checked the Internet and discovered that Nantahala River Rafting has a Web site. You might check that out. Someone there might know his grandpa. I only knew him as Grandpa MacEwen.

If you find Matthew, tell him his old buddy said, "Hi and I'll try to be in touch one of these days."

If you will, let me know how he is.

Sincerely,
Bruce Canton

Christine had checked the Web site, then called and was told that Matthew MacEwen worked there as a white-water instructor. He also led tours at Nantahala, on other rivers in the southeast, and even in other countries.

Christine returned the letter to her purse, wondering if Matthew MacEwen still carried bitterness. Did he blame her for his burned hands?

Bruce Canton said Matthew MacEwen thinks I died. Do I just blurt out, "Hey, I'm alive"? Maybe I should just go home. But having come this far, I have to see him. I have to know what he looks like.

She laid her napkin in her box, closed the lid, and took it to a trash can. Seeing that the golden retriever had disappeared, she quickly rose, wondering if its master had returned. Walking closer, she saw the dog drinking from the river.

Christine approached a woman watching a little boy whose beautiful face was surrounded by bright, rust-colored hair. He stepped from one rock to another in the shallow water at the edge of the river. The woman, with love on her face and in her voice, warned in a soft southern drawl, "Be careful, Simon. The rocks are slippery."

Christine spoke to them and discovered the woman lived in South Carolina. Simon was obviously a tremendous joy to his mom.

After talking with them for awhile, Christine walked

up to the bridge that spanned the river. In the middle were two small lookouts, surrounded by railings, where one could step down and observe without impeding traffic. When a spot opened up, Christine stepped down and held onto the railing as she looked at the river.

Further upstream, children and adults were getting into and out of rafts and kayaks. Was one of them Matthew MacEwen?

One raft holding three adults and two children flowed down the river and under the bridge. Christine moved to the other side of the bridge to watch it flow out of sight. A young boy's kayak stuck in an eddy. He tried to paddle out, but the kayak just kept turning in circles. Not being a salmon, he couldn't maneuver upstream. He was caught in the rapids for quite awhile. Christine wondered where an instructor might be.

Then she realized what she'd already observed. The river was only a few feet deep in that area. He wasn't in danger but was apparently learning how to maneuver in rough water. He never gave up and eventually was able to get the canoe out of the eddy and over to the side. Finally, he paddled downstream like an expert.

What kind of situation have I gotten myself into? Am I like the little boy, going in circles? Will this go smoothly? What do I do? What do I say to Matthew MacEwen? Hey, guess what—I'm the one who ruined your life?

Her watch indicated she still had about thirty minutes before he would arrive. She hurried off the bridge, realizing she hadn't looked toward the dog in quite awhile.

Returning to the picnic area, she breathed a sigh of relief. The dog still lay there. She sat on a bench and stared at it. She'd heard that dogs looked like their masters and often took on their characteristics. She almost laughed to think that Matthew MacEwen looked like a soulful-eyed, long-tongued, long-haired golden retriever who apparently liked the taste of her hands each time she'd bent to pet it.

When she was down to fifteen minutes before Matthew MacEwen might appear, Christine walked over to the dog again. Feelings of anxiety replaced seven years of anticipation. She couldn't just walk up to him and say, "Hi, I'm the girl you rescued."

Most of the people had left. Every once in awhile, a group came out of the center. She watched, but no one went toward the dog or the truck. She'd never been in the mountains before, but from somewhere, perhaps from a book, she had the impression that the sun set early along some mountainsides. This must be one of them. The sky had turned a darker blue and the rays of the sun a deeper gold.

The dog stood, wagging its tail and salivating as if hoping she might do something. She unhooked the chain from around the tree and held onto it as she walked with the dog along the riverside.

A raft stopped where she had seen people unloading earlier. A man and several children got out and went into a building across the river. Was that him? She hurried around to the front of the center, too antsy to stand still, and walked the dog near the truck.

After about ten minutes of pacing back and forth, she saw the screen door open. A tall man in tan slacks and a sienna shirt walked out. He paused on the shadowed porch and looked around.

He focused on her and the dog, then dashed down the steps with the agility of an athlete. He looked like one too, with such an extraordinary build. Hands in his pockets, he took long strides toward her. The slanting rays of the evening sun touched his wet, lion-colored hair, turning it to gold, matching his shirt. Swept back, his hair looked conservatively short surrounding his face and tapered to his collar in back.

As he neared, she studied his features. He was a handsome man with a wide forehead, a straight nose, high cheekbones, full lips forming a taut line, a clearly defined jaw line. His smooth skin displayed a healthy hue beneath the golden tan.

He stood before her, at least a head taller than she. He looked so perfect. Perhaps it was that tall, lean look about him, or the way he held himself, as if set apart, that made him seem more like an artist than a rugged outdoorsman.

Her breath caught. *Yes, he's a golden retriever.*

Is this my rescuer?

The man who risked his life for me?

She couldn't speak, just stared into his face. His gray-green eyes, fringed with dark, golden-brown lashes, narrowed as he looked at her.

She remembered looking into the eyes of the man who rescued her. They had reflected the horror she had felt. Now, they looked at her quizzically. She'd never thought about his looks, only that he must have been an angel.

Matthew MacEwen didn't look like any image she'd ever had of an angel. Instead, he looked incredibly human.

What seemed like an eternity must have been a moment.

"Miss." He glanced down at the dog. "I believe you have something that belongs to me."

Yes, my heart. My eternal gratitude.

"Yes, I. . ." She paused. "While I was waiting, I thought I'd take the dog for a walk."

"Thank you." When he smiled, she was not surprised to note he had perfectly straight white teeth. "Her name is Beauty," he said.

"It fits." She laughed, then her gaze slid from his

face, over his broad shoulders and wide chest, down to his trim waist.

She saw his hands coming out of his pockets. The hands that had slapped the fire out of her hair, had beaten away the flames from her dress burning on her back, had carried her out of the plane.

Bruce Canton had warned her about his burned hands.

She wouldn't look.

But when he reached for the chain, her gaze was drawn to his hands as if they were magnets.

T W O

Christine hated her audible intake of breath. Despite the warning, she was unprepared for the pink scar tissue covering Matthew's gnarled fingers and hands. The tips of some fingers were blunt instead of rounded. Some fingernails were missing.

She would not have reacted had they been anyone else's hands. But she gasped because his disfigurement was a result of his having rescued her. She couldn't tell him that.

How long she stared, she didn't know. But sometimes only a glance could be too long. She looked up at him. The sun still shone on him, but his expression had darkened.

"Here, I'll take the leash." His voice was monotone. She noticed he was careful not to touch her.

Her voice became a whisper. "I'm sorry." Guilt overwhelmed her for gasping at the sight of his hands.

"Forget it," he said. "I'm used to it." He knelt, unfastened the chain from the dog's collar, and said, "Go."

She watched Beauty run off. Christine felt he probably wished she would "go," but she was as bound to her objective as if Matthew MacEwen had the chain fastened around her neck.

He stood, and Christine lifted her gaze. The glow had left his eyes, now shadowed as the sun hid behind a mountain.

"You asked for me?" His voice sounded stiff.

"Yes." He no longer seemed friendly, instead holding himself aloof. She couldn't blame him. She tried to keep her voice from shaking. "I wanted to ask you—"

She couldn't bring herself to ask if he were the one who rescued her. She knew the answer to that. "I want to ask you. . .if you will teach me to. . .raft? Is that what you call it? Go down the river in one of those plastic rafts?"

She wasn't sure if he cleared his throat, coughed, or laughed. He returned to his congenial manner, asking, "Have you ever been in one of those plastic rafts?"

She shook her head. "Never."

"For your information," he said in a friendly way, "they're not plastic. They're rubber."

"Oh," she said. "I've been watching. It doesn't look too difficult."

"With a little instruction," he said, "there's nothing

here to be afraid of, except rocks."

Yes, she feared rocks. The kind of rock-hard expression that would creep into his eyes if she revealed her identity. The rock-hard feeling in his heart when she would tell him she was the reason he paddled down a river instead of presenting his art in exhibits in New York and perhaps all over the world.

She could not blurt out that she was the girl whose life he had saved, in the process losing his future.

Please, know me, like me, before you have to hate me.

In her years of wondering what he was doing, she'd pictured him as being married, having a beautiful wife, wonderful children, a great job. He would be a brave man with tremendous kindness.

She thought his expression now reflected a touch of impatience. However, he wasn't telling her to get lost. "If you need to go home or anything," she said, "I can come back in the morning."

One of his eyebrows twitched slightly at that. "No one's waiting for me," he said. His lips pressed together as if trying to suppress a smile. Did he think she was flirting with him? He looked toward Slow Joe's. "I'd like to get something to eat."

Feeling relief, she nodded. Her emotions flipped between gratitude that he would stay and talk with her and sorrow that apparently no loving wife or children were waiting for him.

"Excuse me," he said. "I want to put the chain in the truck."

Christine walked ahead to one of the picnic tables.

"Do you want anything?" Matthew asked, when he came over.

"I've already eaten, but I'll have a cup of water."

"I'll get it," he said.

Only a few people remained in the area. Two families sat at tables. A couple of guys at another. One family stood on the porch ordering. A little boy looked at Matthew's hands, then raised his head to look into Matthew's face.

Matthew said, "Hi, Buddy."

The little boy said, "Hi." He looked at the hands again, then turned toward his parents as if nothing had taken place.

Why couldn't I have done that?

She answered her own question. *Because I'm not an innocent child. My seven-year expectations are not being met the way I'd dreamed.*

Matthew returned with a couple of bean, meat, and cheese burritos and two cups. He set her water in front of her.

Without thinking, she said, "Thank you, Matthew."

He swung his long legs over the bench and sat, asking, "And you are—?"

Christine grasped the foam cup tightly, forcing the sides together so that water and chipped ice spilled over the top. Suppose he asked how she knew his name? What would she say?

A breathless moment passed. She'd like to be that splash of water disappearing down the gap between the table boards. She reached for a napkin and swiped the ice off the table, saying, "I'm such a klutz."

"I can get you more water."

"That's okay. There's plenty of ice in the cup."

She looked over at him. Did she imagine an icy expression in his eyes?

❧   ❧   ❧

Matthew saw the fear in her eyes and the color drain from her face before she dumped her water on the table. Had she been afraid he might reach out his hand to shake hers when he had asked her name?

He knew better than to offer his hand. He had the kind of hands that in movies made people shriek and run away in terror. He was grateful he had the use of them. But he never ceased to be sensitive about touching another person.

Asking to move his church membership from Atlanta five years ago, he'd stood in front of the congregation at the little mountain church where his grandpa had worshiped. People were invited to come by and welcome him into their fellowship and shake his hands.

He knew that Christians had the same emotions as unbelievers and had kept his hands clasped at his waist in full view. He only unclasped them when others extended their hands first. Men apparently had no problem with it. A few women offered their hand, some laid their hand on his, some took hold of his arm in a warm gesture.

One boy, about twelve years old, stuck his hand out, challenge in his eyes. He squeezed hard. "Did that hurt?" he asked. Thinking the boy wanted it to, Matthew replied, "You're strong, that's for sure."

The boy's face brightened, even as the adult with him apologized. Matthew didn't mind. Children were curious, but none ever ran away screaming; and after a long look, they didn't really seem to care what his hands looked like.

Most of the time, Matthew accepted what couldn't be changed and went on with his life. Occasionally, on a day like today, he was overly sensitive because emotions he had suppressed threatened to surface and he could wish he might hold this young woman's soft hands in his.

Were he able, he would love to capture on canvas

her delicate facial features, long dark lashes that complimented her fair skin, dainty nose, high cheekbones, and full, naturally pink lips. An artist's challenge would be her medium brown eyes that expressed a gamut of emotion—delight, uncertainty, shock, chagrin, curiosity, reserve, revulsion—in the few moments since he'd encountered her.

She stirred his curiosity as the cool breeze stirred her long, straight, fine hair, so dark it was almost black. When she bowed her head while wiping up the spilled water, her hair fell forward, gently caressing her cheeks. Her hair and eyes reflected a touch of gold borrowed from the setting sun.

He would paint her against a background of—

Matthew forced away those thoughts. He had to stop thinking—feeling—like an artist. She'd rather spill her water than chance his touch.

He removed the paper from the straw and poked it into his milkshake. "You might tell me your name."

"Christine," she said. "Christine Norwood."

Something about the way she said it made him wonder if he should know her. Her voice was hesitant but at the same time sounded like some famous actor might say, "Bond. James Bond."

She was pretty enough and elegant enough to be a famous actress or model. However, he knew the names of very few, not being the type of person who idolized another human being, although he could appreciate good acting if done in a decent movie.

Two people in his life who'd meant the most to him wouldn't be considered physically attractive. One, his grandpa, a man weathered by time and with mannerisms city folk would consider rough as the bark on a tree. He'd died at the ripe old age of ninety-three. Another had been a physical therapist, a big-boned woman with buck teeth and beady eyes. She'd had faith and determination that he'd regain use of his fingers. Her attitude had eventually transferred to Matthew.

Although he told himself physical attraction wasn't the most important thing, by anyone's standards this young woman sitting across from him was lovely, like a delicate flower. Willie had said a real pretty girl had asked for him a couple of hours ago. Since she knew his name, likely someone had recommended him, or she'd seen his name in one of the brochures. This was business. Only business. He swallowed a bite of burrito, then asked, "Have you ever rafted or canoed or kayaked?"

"No, but I've swum in pools, in lakes, in the ocean and have even tried my hand—" She grinned. "Or I should say 'I tried my feet' at surfing. Wasn't too successful."

"Due to your accent and your, um. . ." He grinned at

her. "Your. . .knowledge of rafting, I'd say you're not from around here."

"San Diego. I lived with my grandparents. My parents died when I was young."

"I'm sorry," he said. He could truly empathize, having lost his grandparents and lived away from his parents much of his life. "You have relatives in this area?"

"No." She shook her head and looked uncomfortable, toying with her cup. He guessed she didn't want to talk about personal details. After a moment she said, "I'm interested in rafting."

He nodded. *Keep it businesslike.* "The river has a life of its own. You can't tame it. You just learn to go with the flow."

"That sounds challenging."

"It's a challenge, all right. And you never dare it. It will win."

"That was my first lesson, I guess?" She lifted the cup to her generously curved lips.

"Free of charge," he said and smiled. After a studied look, he added, "Sounds to me like you might be looking for a one-day thrill."

"What?" She apparently swallowed a piece of ice. She gulped and put her hand on her throat.

THREE

Matthew stifled a laugh at her priceless look of surprise. "Sorry," he said. "I forget some people don't know the lingo here. What I mean is, you would probably like the Paddling Sampler. Our brochures describe various river courses. The adventure for those just looking for a day of fun is referred to as 'a one-day thrill.'"

"Oh." Color blushed her cheeks. "Okay. Sounds intriguing. What does it entail?"

Matthew explained. "You start out on the lake and you learn the basics. You need to master the technique of paddling before you're ready for any of the crafts."

"You mean I sit in the river and practice paddling?"

"No, no. You sit in a canoe."

"Whew." She made a gesture of wiping sweat from her forehead. "You had me worried."

He took a bite of his burrito, intrigued by the way she sort of ducked her head as if embarrassed. However, she grinned when she admitted, "I'm inexperienced."

"Right," he said, as if he hadn't already deduced that. "You can get instruction pamphlets from the center that outline what we have to offer. We have classic courses, canoeing, playboating, river running, rolling, creek technique. . . ."

She nodded. "Do you offer private instruction?"

"The center does. It all depends on what you want, how much time it takes. I suppose anything's possible for a price."

She picked up her cup and took a sip of water. How people dressed at the river—generally short, cut-off denims, jeans, T-shirts, even bathing suits—gave no indication of the size of their bank accounts. However, judging from the expensive look of her slacks and shirt, he felt she'd have no problem paying for private instructions.

He'd just thrust the last bite of the burrito into his mouth when she asked, "Could I hire you for a. . .um. . . one-day thrill?"

He pointed to his mouth, indicating he needed to chew before answering. He needed to think—to handle this right. He swallowed and washed his burrito down with milkshake.

Was she flirting with him? Looking at her face, he

didn't think so. A light shade of pink had colored her cheeks. Her warm brown eyes held an expression of uncertainty. Her smile seemed tentative, rather like the Mona Lisa. Was she bold? Was she shy?

She quickly looked away from his gaze, and he saw her swallow hard. He felt she might even cry if he turned her down. She had spoken boldly, but he detected a vulnerability about her.

"I don't do this every day," he explained. "I book trips for a few people who know me and vacation here each summer. Most of my participants are experienced. Later this summer I'll be white-water kayaking for seven days in Costa Rica with a group of ten participants."

Her look of interest presented a challenge. He could work her in if he wanted, and the thought of it appealed to him. He would like to sit in a two-person kayak with her while they paddled down the river, then he would take her through the rapids. Although he knew to respect the river, he was good at what he did. While his hands didn't look like much, on the river, others could admire how functional they were. But he'd decided long ago that trying to prove anything to anybody served no purpose. Why get himself into a situation that could cause him distress?

The way she traced the rim of her foam cup with her index finger and looked thoughtfully at it indicated to him she was disappointed. He could almost believe she wanted to be with him in particular.

But he could recommend several other good instructors. Apparently he needed to drive his point home. "I'm busy all this week. I teach basics to young people from an area camp. I have a different group each day according to their ability. Some are disabled."

"Oh, that's so kind of you." Christine looked at him with such admiration, he felt he might do something he didn't think he'd ever done—blush.

"It's the least I can do," Matthew said. "I want these young people to know that a disability doesn't mean the end of the world. They can do many worthwhile things."

"Matthew, could I go on one of those trips with you? Maybe I could help. I don't care about just having fun."

"Sorry," he said. "The basic requirement is that you have fun."

"Okay," she said. He loved her smile. Then it vanished. She spoke seriously. "I really would like to help, if I can."

The camp would never turn down someone with proper credentials. And if she were an experienced rafter, he and the camp director would readily accept her. Matthew shook his head. "These campers are burn survivors."

The way she closed her eyes for a moment and the

nod of her head indicated that should be a foregone conclusion.

She opened her eyes and looked over at him then. "Look, Matthew. I know I must look like some weirdo to you."

He certainly wouldn't place her in the weirdo-looking category. Anything but! However, he couldn't quite figure her out. He turned up his cup and filled his mouth with milkshake instead of responding. Too cold! If he wasn't careful, he'd get an ice-cream headache. He felt like his throat was freezing. Too bad his emotions weren't.

"You see. . ." She appeared to search for the right words. "I really would like to help. I'm here for a purpose, although I can't talk about it right now. I'm trying to find what worthwhile thing God has for me to do in this world. Something like. . ."

Her voice trailed off, and she took a deep breath. Matthew stared at her as she tried to keep her composure. He felt she was sincere. "You're a Christian?"

"Yes." She sounded confident about that. "I am a believer." She looked down then. "And I'm trying to learn how to follow."

Been there, done that—and still trying. He could almost laugh at the irony. Here he was struggling with personal thoughts about this girl and dealing with what might have been, what couldn't be, what if, and all those other phrases connected with that word "if." Then she puts everything on a spiritual basis.

Way to go, God!

FOUR

Matthew wasn't sure if his response was personal or spiritual. However, he decided to make an exception in Christine's case. After all, since she had brought God into the situation, it took on a different appearance. Or should!

"Tell you what," he said. "If you'll be here in the morning before nine o'clock, and if there's enough room in one of the rafts for you, I'll ask the camp leader if you can join us. Now, this is unorthodox, so don't be surprised if the answer is no."

"I'll be here before nine o'clock."

He thought he'd been surprised enough for one day until she added, "Could you recommend someplace I might stay? A hotel or a cabin or something?"

She didn't even have a place to stay! He wondered if she were hiding out. Running from somebody. Or just a rich girl bored with life, looking for adventure. He wadded up his napkin and dropped it into the foam container. "We have lodging here, usually shared cabins. You get to know other students."

She shook her head. "I'd rather have private lodging in a hotel or a cabin by myself."

"How long do you plan to stay?"

She shrugged. "I can't say yet."

He thought for a moment. "I can show you a place you might like."

"Perfect," she said. Her beautiful brown eyes held the expression of a young child anticipating Christmas. Her soft pink lips spread in a lovely smile, as if she were a woman who liked the man sitting across from her.

Matthew crunched another chip in his mouth, closed the foam container, grabbed his milkshake, and heard the slurp of his straw as it hit bottom. He gathered his trash.

Concern sounded in her voice. "Matthew, I don't want you to go out of your way."

"It's no trouble, Christine." She visibly relaxed when he smiled at her. "I do happen to pass the lodging on the way to my home."

He whistled, and Beauty came running, looking up at him with her tongue hanging out and her eyes big and round, trusting and hoping, as if he had a dog biscuit in his pocket. And, of course, he did. He reached into his pocket and drew out a biscuit. "Get in the truck and it's all yours."

"Amazing," Christine said when the dog trotted along beside him, then jumped into the back of the truck.

Matthew threw in the biscuit, laughing. "Not really. It's routine, and Beauty's a glutton."

A short while later, Matthew looked in his rearview mirror. He did that often when Beauty was in the back of the truck. This time, his gaze moved beyond Beauty to the car trailing him.

Not since college days had a pretty girl followed him.

A thought of irony struck him. Not only was Christine following him, she was willing to pay for his company.

Get real, Matthew!

ᴣ   ᴣ   ᴣ

Christine reached the center at 8:45 A.M. and parked beside Matthew's truck. Beauty, in the back of the truck, wagged her tail in greeting as if Christine were an old friend. Matthew leaned out the window as she approached.

Walking up to him, she stifled a yawn. "Oh, excuse me."

"What this?" he said. "Did Mountain View give you a lumpy mattress?"

She cast a disdainful gaze at the clear blue sky, already brightened by the sun. "Do you know it's 5:45 California time? I haven't quite adjusted to the time change."

"Since you're up," he said, "you'd better hop in or they'll leave without us."

She looked at the river and back at him. "Hop in?"

He chuckled. "In the truck. We put in from the Nantahala Gorge, eight miles up the road."

She drew in her breath. "Then I can go?"

He frowned and sounded doubtful. "We'll find out when we get there."

"If—" She hesitated. "If I can't, how do I get back down here?"

"It's only eight miles. You can hike, can't you?" His eyes began to twinkle with humor. "Or sometimes, if the group is small and the children beg hard enough, I take Beauty along. I might have to decide which I chain to a tree—you or Beauty."

She playfully hit his arm. "You keep that up and I may have to take one of those paddles to you."

"Get in," he said playfully.

Walking around the truck, a shiver of delight raced through her. She recalled a saying she hoped was true—people only tease people they like.

She hopped up into the truck and fastened the seat belt. "Actually," she said, as he backed out of the parking lot, "I woke up several times during the night, excited about this trip, hoping I could tag along."

"I called the director last night," he confessed. "It's fine if you go."

He pulled out onto the highway. "How do you like Mountain View?"

Last night, when he'd taken her there, she had expressed her delight with the picture-perfect setting of a small village. Back from a rustic wooden fence stood charming, quaint cottages set against a background of high mountain peaks.

"I love the little cottage," she said. She hadn't minded the cottages being rented only by the week or month. She'd taken it for a week. The hardwood floors, small kitchen-dining area adjoining the living room, bathroom, and one bedroom suited her purposes just fine. "I even have a small deck from where I can look out at Fontana Lake."

Soon he was telling her about the river. "The upper Nantahala flows into the lower Nantahala at the gorge. They're separated by a power station. My grandpa took me on trips down the river before I could even walk." He grinned. "Around here, when someone talks about the Nanny, they're not referring to a baby-sitter."

When they pulled in at the "put in," the group of children paid Christine no mind, instead squealing and pulling at the wagging tail of Beauty when she ran up to them.

"This is Christine," Matthew said. "She'll be joining us."

The adults introduced themselves—Meg, Jason, Mark, Len, and Traci.

"Thanks so much for letting me go with you," Christine said.

"You're welcome," said the middle-aged man called Len. He had raised scars on his neck and under his chin that curved onto his jaw. "Any friend of Matt's is a friend of ours."

Traci looked skeptical. "That's a beautiful outfit. Makes the rest of us look kinda grungy."

Mark yelled out, "Speak for yourself, Traci."

They all laughed. Christine explained. "I haven't had a chance to shop yet. I only brought two outfits with me. This is what I wore all day yesterday, so I might look good, but at least I can smell bad. How's that?"

Traci nodded approvingly. "Perfect. Welcome to the club."

"All right," Matthew said. "You guys go in and get your equipment. I'll get Beauty chained up and meet you where we put in."

Len took Christine's arm. "Let me introduce you to our kids."

He called them each by name. One little boy had no hair on one side of his head and a lump of tissue where an ear should be. The tips of three fingers and fingernails were missing from another boy's hands. A little blond girl in long braids had scars on her face. Several children's arms or legs were injured. Christine didn't see any scars on the boy in long pants, who used crutches.

The one who touched Christine's heart the most was a frail child named Chloe, who looked to be around eight. The morning breeze parted her bangs, revealing raised scars across her forehead and on her face, giving the impression she wore a corrugated mask. Behind thick-lens glasses, she stared at Christine with dark, sad eyes surrounded by pink, raised flesh. Christine could only assume the girl would have many more surgeries. It was a miracle she could see at all.

As soon as they were introduced, the children ran, walked fast, or limped toward the building. Chloe seemed reluctant. Traci called her, "Come on, Chloe."

Chloe took a deep breath. Christine thought she might be scared. Christine bent down and said in a whisper, "You know what? I've never rafted before. If it's allowed, would you save me a place by you?"

Chloe's big brown eyes brightened. She nodded and almost smiled.

Traci held out her hand, and Chloe reached up with hers. Christine's smile widened when she saw Chloe tilt her face toward Traci and say, "She wants to sit by me."

Matthew walked up. He had apparently heard Chloe's words as well. Christine felt like she could melt under the warmth in his gray-green eyes when he smiled and said, "Looks like you made a friend."

Christine nodded. "I hope so."

She wasn't thinking only of Chloe. Len had said a friend of Matthew's was a friend of theirs. She wanted to be Matthew's friend. *Oh, please let that happen.*

☤ ☤ ☤

They stood near the rafts where they would put into the river, listening to safety instructions. Matthew said helmets weren't necessary on this section of the Nantahala. It was to be a relaxing float with mild rapids. But all had to wear life jackets. "Down close to the center, the rafts will sit near the bottom of the river. In other places the water is six-to-seven feet deep. It's not likely anyone will fall out, but it has happened. You need to know the white-water swim position to avoid foot entrapment."

He explained that if they fell out, they should float on their back with their feet up to the surface. If they tried to stand, they could get a foot wedged in the rocks on the bottom. "That's a dangerous thing in the rapids. Now, for paddling."

Remembering her earlier comment, Christine glanced at Matthew. He must have remembered, too. He gave her a warning look, then grinned. He held a paddle and explained the "all forward, left forward, and right forward" paddling stroke commands. "Let me warn you. You'll get a cold splash. The water temperature is around fifty-four degrees."

Christine didn't see that it mattered. The day was warm, and she'd probably work up a sweat paddling.

"Those of you who haven't rafted before might want to sit in back of the raft," Matthew said. "The more experienced or braver ones who don't mind getting wet and like roller coasters sit up front."

Christine hated roller coasters and didn't feel brave. She doubted she could float without trying to stand on that rocky bottom if she fell out. Feeling a hand on hers, she looked down at Chloe, who was looking up at her. Good. She'd sit in back with this shy little girl.

"You can sit with me," Chloe said. "I've rafted before."

The little girl climbed in front, and Christine had no choice but to join her. Soon after they were on the river and she'd barely had time to obey the paddling commands, Matthew warned they were headed for Patton's Run.

The roller-coaster ride began.

Chloe's shrill scream brought out the maternal instinct in Christine, until she realized the little girl was having the time of her life. When the raft tilted up in front, Christine opened her mouth to scream; but by that time it had dropped, and she got a mouthful of water and a face-washing.

Christine decided to breathe again as they came out of the rapids and paddled along calmer water. Matthew had them paddle their rafts close to each other.

His voice, clear as the water and the sky, resonated in the pristine setting. "Nantahala," he said, "was named by the Cherokee Indians. There's a reservation near here where you can visit the Oconoluftee Indian Village. Many things of interest are there, including their museum. You can see basket weaving going on. Nantahala means 'Land of the Noonday Sun.' These mountains shut out the sunlight in much of Nantahala. One of the shaded trails is the Appalachian Trail. It crosses the river at the footbridge up behind the center where we finish today."

Christine settled into the calm float, drifting with the flow of the river, when Chloe poked her leg with her finger. "Listen," the girl said, her eyes wide behind her glasses.

The roar of the rapids became louder, reminding Christine of a waterfall. Surely not! Just then, Matthew loudly announced they were coming to Nantahala Falls. The roar of the rapids competed with his voice. "This one is longer than Patton's Run. You'll have about a five-foot drop. Just hang in there, and I'll see you at the bottom."

This time, the roller coaster seemed to have come unhinged. Not only was it longer than Patton's Run, the ride was faster. The sides of the raft bent, and the front lifted toward the sky. Christine screamed along with the others. Suddenly they dropped and were splashed so completely she thought they'd turned over. However, due to no expertise of anyone in the raft, it settled innocently on the water as if the wild ride had never happened.

She hadn't lost her life, and her foot wasn't on the bottom of the river, caught between rocks.

With her hair dripping down her shivering body, Christine, chilled to the bone, hugged her arms. Now that the scare had ended, the joy of the adventure swept over her, and she yearned for more.

Around 12:30 they reached the center. By that time she'd almost dried out, but she knew she must look like she'd gone through a washing machine. She felt like it.

While the children and counselors ate lunch at Slow Joe's, Christine drove Matthew and Len to the gorge for the truck and the camp bus.

After they returned, Christine and Matthew ate lunch together.

"Well, how did you like it?" he asked.

She knew she looked bedraggled, but she felt exhilarated. "It's the wildest thing I've ever done. I know that paddle must be permanently notched with my fingerprints."

He laughed.

Since he was in such a jovial mood, she asked, "Could I go again tomorrow? Please?"

FIVE

Tomorrows came and went for the rest of the week.

Anxiety accompanied Christine's anticipation on the last day. What would she do when this day ended?

She'd loved the routine of rafting each morning with the camp staff and children, then her and Matthew having lunch together at Slow Joe's. On the ride in the truck from the center to the gorge, she and Matthew were unusually silent. Did he wonder, too, what might come next?

On the river, however, there was no time for reflections, just fun and frivolity. The same camp leaders had gone each day but had taken a different group of children. Today was for the teens. Christine whooped and hollered with them as if they were at a football game.

When they floated into the seven-foot-deep water, Matthew mentioned that some rafters often took a swim there. A boy stood, lost his balance, and fell out of the raft.

Christine yelled, "I'll save you," and jumped in.

"I'm okay," he said, looking fearful of reprimand, while treading water.

"I know," she said, loud enough for the others to hear. "I just thought this was a great way to get my bath and do my laundry at the same time."

"Oh, no," Matthew groaned when the others took that as a cue to follow her and the boy's examples. "If you can't beat them, join them," he jumped in.

When they climbed back in, Matthew warned, "No more accidental falls. The river is shallower from here on down, and you'd get scraped by the rocks."

That trip took three hours instead of the usual two and a half.

After the teens and staff all said their good-byes, Matthew looked wistfully at their bus as it pulled away. "That's over until next year."

"You really love the river, don't you?" she asked needlessly. She knew Matthew felt at home on the river. She'd loved watching the excitement in his eyes as he conquered the rapids and delighted in the children.

"It's a lesson in life each time I go out," he said. "My grandpa said that life is like the river—ups and downs, rapid and slow. Sometimes you get hit in the face with it, sometimes completely doused with icy cold water. It's rocky. It's smooth. He emphasized that without a competent guide, the raft will slam into the boulders, causing injury or death. He related that to God as our Guide. Without Him, we can't navigate safely through the dangers and over the rough spots. Those are facts."

Facts of life, yes, and Christine had watched Matthew forget everything else but the river and the people. She'd seen his complete concentration and delight. On the river, he hadn't been self-conscious about his hands. They were part of his expertise—strong and everyone could trust them in that situation.

What about the rest of the time—on land?

Christine and Matthew threw away their lunch containers.

He whistled for Beauty.

Now what? Was it time to blurt out her identity?

He put his hands in his pockets. Was he preparing to say good-bye. . .without shaking hands?

Should she leave?

No, she still had to find out if she could help him in any way. If there was anything she could do for him to express her thanks. Did he need anything? Rafting probably didn't pay a big salary.

She didn't want to say anything to turn the joy of the river adventure to despair. How could she say, "I'm the one who hurt you, who destroyed your future"? She couldn't.

Wanting to break the awkward silence, she said, "Oh, I didn't pay for the trips."

"My treat," he replied. "You were a big help. And fun."

"Thank you." She needed to let him know how she felt without saying too much. "I really loved it. The children were wonderful."

"On the river, they discover we're all alike. We're not burn victims. We're just people who got burned." He glanced at Beauty, who waited for the command so she could have her treat. "I don't have anything booked for a couple of weeks. So, if you're interested in further instruction—"

Christine glanced at Beauty. This was tricky. She'd like that, but what she had to say mustn't be said on the river.

"Or," he said, before she'd decided how to respond, "if you're still in the area Sunday, I'd like to invite you to attend my church."

"Thank you," she said. "I'd love to."

       ଧ   ଧ   ଧ

"Good morning," Matthew said in greeting that Sunday.

Wow! What a day. Only midmorning and blessings abounded. The setting was superb. Christine stood at the railing on the wooden lookout near her cottage, gazing down upon the trees that stretched out to the sun-touched Fontana Lake. A pleasant rain had fallen during the night. She'd been up early enough to see the clouds caress the mountaintops and the mist rise from the forest floor.

The rain had cooled the air, making it crisp and fresh.

Now, another blessing had walked up beside her and said, "Good morning," in a way that warmed her more than the steamy double mocha cappuccino that she held tightly. Hold tightly was what she tried to do with her emotions upon looking at him.

The golden retriever stood beside her. And she wasn't thinking of the dog. Matthew took her breath away. The morning sun splashed him with gold. His eyes were green as the lime-colored linen shirt he wore with bone-colored pants.

"You look sharp," she said.

He tilted his head in a rakish manner. "If one can't be the sharpest knife in the drawer, he can at least dress sharp. Frankly, I was trying to match the style I expected of you."

"You said anything goes since this is a tourist area," she said. "I hope this is all right."

His glance swept over her light blue silk pants, silk and spandex top, and the lightweight jacket she could take off when the day warmed. His green eyes sparked with a glint of golden sun. "You don't have a thing to be concerned about, except approving stares."

Oh, she wanted to fall into his arms and have him hold her and kiss her and never, never let her go. Thankfully she had self-discipline in action, if not in thought.

"I've already determined," she said, "that TV has a stereotypical way of portraying mountain people. But I haven't seen a single. . . What do you call them? Hayseeds?"

"Nah," he said. "I think that's country bumpkins. In the mountains it's hillbillies."

She shrugged. "I haven't run into any *Deliverance* characters."

"There are all kinds of people everywhere," he said. "But the kind of deliverance I'm interested in is what the Lord does for us sinful creatures."

She thought he was appealing before. What in the world could attract her more than a charming man who had a strong Christian faith?

She could think of nothing!

ଯ   ଯ   ଯ

Instead of the truck, Matthew led her to a late model, sand-colored sports car. That surprised her. She didn't expect a rafting instructor to have a lot of money. Maybe he borrowed it. Or rented it. Anyway, the car was sleek, and he drove like he owned it.

He parked in a gravel lot next to a pretty little white frame building with a steeple on top. The church she attended in San Diego was a large, two-story brick building with a fellowship hall in the basement.

Upon entering the sanctuary, Christine returned the friendly smiles. Matthew led her down the single aisle to a pew several rows from the back. Immediately women introduced themselves and men extended their hands in welcome.

As the notes sounded on the piano, the congregation grew silent and a man with rolled-up shirtsleeves welcomed visitors and made announcements. "Let's stand and sing," he then said, giving the number of a hymn in the songbooks scattered across pews that she noted were not padded like those at her church in California.

Her home church also had stained-glass windows. This church instead had clear glass-paned windows, raised to let in the cool mountain breeze or maybe to let out the heartfelt singing of voices that held back nothing. The congregation sang with all their might, untrained except by the Holy Spirit.

Christine was accustomed to hearing trained voices, led by a professional choir director called a minister of music. She could readily see that her church was not better, just different.

She and Matthew held the same hymnbook. She wanted to move her hand and let it touch his. She wanted to feel those hands that saved her life. But he kept his fingers on the edge of the hymnal, as far as possible from her.

My voice is blending with that of my hero, the one who saved my life, while we're acknowledging the One who saved our souls. She feared she might cry.

She knew that Scripture, "No greater love has a man than he lay down his life for his friends." Jesus had laid His life down willingly. He had saved her soul.

But while Matthew had saved her life, he hadn't willingly given up his future life in the art world. That had been an unasked-for, tragic result.

In one sense, she could feel incredibly blessed that her soul and life had been saved. In another sense, she agonized for Matthew. He was a part of her life. But if he knew that their relationship truly began seven years ago, if he knew who she really was, would this wonderful dream turn out to be a nightmare in progress?

After church, before he started the car, Matthew turned toward her. "Would you like to get a bite to eat? Being tourist season, the nicer places will be filled. But if you don't mind the possibility of having to wait a short while, the food will be worth it."

Another idea began to form in her mind. "Why don't we just stop at a fast-food place? A grilled chicken sandwich would suit me just fine."

They sat at a small table for two inside the Chicken Place and soon began exchanging stories about their grandparents. His were no longer living. She called hers each weekend.

After returning to the car, Christine said, "Matthew. You know where I live. Could I see where you live?"

SIX

Matthew stopped at an intersection, with his left blinker turned on. "The road to the right," he said, "leads to the university where I teach."

"Teach?"

She stared at him. He glanced at her and back at the traffic. "You sound like I said that in a foreign language."

Her laugh was short. "No, I just thought you were a rafting instructor."

"You may notice I'm not there today."

"Hmm. You may be right," she said. "What do you teach?"

"Art."

Christine quickly turned her head away from him. A feeling of chagrin washed over her. A writing instructor had said, "If you can't write—teach." Did the same principle hold for an artist? If you can't paint—teach?

She forced her thoughts back to positive things, like the wonderful man beside her and the panoramic view of the mountains.

Matthew handled the sports car around the sweeping curves like he handled the raft on the river—expertly. When they neared the top of the mountain, there was no other traffic.

Small trees and bushes hugged the one-lane road. Massive trees with overhanging limbs made a protective canopy, shutting out the sun. "I've never seen so many trees in one place," she exclaimed.

"Western North Carolina has a greater variety of trees and plants than any other place in the world," he said, "except China."

The sight took her breath away. As they came out of the shade and into the sunlight, she saw a picture-perfect chalet with the rugged mountain as its back-drop. Matthew drove up the paved drive bordered by a rustic wooden fence. He parked underneath a deck, beside his truck. Beauty ran to meet them. Christine leaned over to stroke her long hair.

From the deck, the view was even more spectacular. She'd come from sea level to the top of the world. Once he knew the truth about her, she would go down again.

How?

With a big splash that might turn her upside down, inside out?

Was there a way to come through this and float smoothly as if on calm water?

Pushing aside her trepidation, she followed Matthew through the main floor. She loved the combination of charm and elegance. The living room was furnished with earth-colored, overstuffed, masculine-looking furniture. She'd love to curl up on the big sofa in front of a fire in the wintertime.

The living room was open to the dining area and kitchen. Wood-paneled walls, a stone fireplace, and hardwood floors with rugs lent a cozy ambiance to the rooms. Behind the kitchen lay a bedroom and bath. He led her up the stairs, where a second bedroom and bath were situated behind the loft, which served as his office. Christine stood at the white railing surrounding the loft and looked down into the living room.

A fan hung on a long chain from the tip of the wooden-beamed cathedral ceiling. "It's very beautiful, Matthew," she could honestly say. "You live here alone?"

When he nodded, she ventured further. "You've. . . never been married?"

"No," he said. "My mom and dad, who are missionaries in Korea, stay here when on furlough. Also my sister, who teaches in Korea." He led her back into the kitchen and fixed ice water for them. "This was my grandparents' home. My grandmother died over twenty years ago. Grandpa spent more and more time at his cabin. During the winters he and I usually stayed here. Anyway, he left this to me."

They walked back out onto the deck and sat in wooden chairs. She thought he must be lonely. An unbelievable thought struck her. "Matthew, don't you have a girlfriend?"

"Not seriously since college. She was a junior and I was a senior. We discussed marriage. She talked about the possibility of transferring to New York for her senior year while I attended art school. That summer I was in a plane crash and my hands got burned. She came to see me in the hospital. The first time she was loving and emotional. The next time, when it became clear I wouldn't be going to New York for a long time, if ever, and would definitely have scarred hands, she was sympathetic."

He stopped talking for a moment and took a sip of his water. His voice showed no emotion. She wondered how he really felt.

"On the third visit," he continued, "she revealed her desire not to make any major change, but to finish her education at the area university. She sent a letter later, telling me she was sorry she hadn't been to see me, but schoolwork was so demanding. After that, I received a card with a quick note. It sounded to me like, 'Having a great time. Glad you're not here.' She got married that summer."

So, Christine thought, *I'm responsible for that, too. Even more reason for him to resent me when he knows who I am.*

"Then there was the recuperation," he said. "Operations. Skin grafts. Physical therapy. At a time when I should have been helping my grandparents, they took me in and helped me. I could do nothing with my hands. Imagine one day, an hour, even a few minutes without the use of your hands."

Christine didn't want to. But the ideas surfaced. The simple things one couldn't do. The more humiliating ones. No, she didn't want to imagine what it was like.

He spoke as if that time were a distant memory. But those experiences were vivid to her.

"As soon as I was able, I concentrated on strengthening my hands and completing graduate studies. I took an overload during the school year and extra courses during the summer. I've now completed my third year of teaching. My grandpa's having retired from the university as a history teacher likely worked in my favor in getting a job teaching art. I'm grateful." He glanced over at her. "And to think, without that plane crash, I might have been off with fame and fortune and pride and self-importance.

Instead, I'm this sweet, humble guy. . . ."

He laughed, so she made an effort to join him.

He jested about being a wonderful man, but she thought the description accurate. He might have gained fame and fortune, but she knew he would still have been a kind, self-sacrificing Christian man, like he had been seven years ago when he gave up so much for her.

"And you?" Matthew asked.

"Sure," Christine said. "I'm sweet and humble, too." They both laughed.

"I mean," he said, "do you have a boyfriend?"

"I've had them, but I've never been serious. I always felt I needed to find God's purpose for my life before I would be ready to be committed to a guy."

"Love waits for that?" he asked.

Christine felt the color rise to her face. But Matthew had talked personally. So would she. "I've never been in love."

She pushed aside the word "before" and told herself that it had no place in her confession.

"Anyway," she continued quickly, "my grandparents and my church did a number on me. They stressed the difference between being in love with love and being in love with a person. And I need to feel like the person for me is not just who I want, but who God wants for my life as well."

"You're young to have so strong a faith."

She shook her head. "After losing my parents at an early age, I was never young again."

Warmth shone in his green eyes. He nodded. "I understand. When I was in college, I had the world on a string and the string around my finger. In that world, I believed in God, Jesus, the Holy Spirit, and I planned to let Them have a part in my life. But God wasn't my top priority."

"He is now?"

Matthew took a long moment to answer. His expression was serious. "Let's say, I want Him to be. I still have a long way to go."

She smiled. "That's what my grandparents still say, and they're wonderful Christians."

"Just like you."

"The Christian part, yes." She grinned at him. "The wonderful part is not for me to say."

"I suspect you're wonderful," he returned immediately, which caused her heart to somersault. But they were just being playful. Checking each other out, like Beauty when she sniffed at the hands of those who sought to pet her.

The hands. Christine drew in a deep breath and faced the view.

He spoke softly. "Christine, is there something troubling you?"

She nodded.

"If you care to tell me, I'll listen, even if I can't help."

"I know you would. But I can't talk about it right now."

"That's fine," he said. "Just know I'm here."

Oh, she knew that, in every fiber of her being—in a way she'd never known a man's nearness before.

Christine made herself concentrate on her reason for being in North Carolina. She'd wanted to thank her rescuer and discover if she could do anything for him.

"Matthew, this is a beautiful place to live. You seem to have a full life. Are you happy?"

"Happy?" he said in a way that made her wonder if he thought she'd spoken a foreign language. "I've learned to be content. Oh, I'm aware of the ideal. It would be nice to go home to the love of my life, have her meet me at the door, and smell supper cooking." He grinned. "But I know how much fantasy there is in thoughts like that. I'm very much aware of reality. And I don't mind living alone. Just me and Beauty." He picked up his glass and sipped his water. He set it down again, saying, "But that's enough about me. What are your goals?"

Christine couldn't say everything that was on her heart and in her mind. She couldn't tell him that she would like to travel around and make speeches and tell young people they could go through adversity, lose loved ones, have setbacks, and through it all find a deeper relationship with God. It didn't really make sense, except she'd lived it. She'd done it. She wasn't even sure she could be brave enough to speak to groups. She'd given some presentations at church, but those were in front of her friends, who knew something of her struggles. They'd prayed for her.

"I'm not sure," Christine said finally. "I have registered for graduate studies in English, with a concentration in literature. I feel I'm not very good at communicating, so I majored in English. And literature teaches so much about life. Just one book encompasses a world of wisdom and advice and things you can learn from and impart to others."

"Sounds like you might have a bent toward teaching."

"I don't think I'd do well in a classroom day in and day out," she countered.

"Oh, I see," Matthew said. "You're independently wealthy."

She squinted her eyes, trying to look offended. "But you know what the Good Book says. To she who much is given, much is required."

"Definitely a paraphrase, but tell me, if you could do anything in the world, what would it be?"

She couldn't say her goal for seven years had been to find her rescuer, thank him, and help him in any way possible. But he had a teaching job, his summers of rafting, which he obviously loved, a home, a truck, a car, a dog. Did he want more?

She walked over to the railing and leaned back against it. "Could I see your etchings?"

"Etchings?" He cast her a look of skepticism.

"You did say you teach art. Surely, with this glorious setting, you must paint, too."

"Only at Cataloochee."

"Cat-a-who-chy?"

He laughed. "Cataloochee. It's a valley and forest near here. My grandpa's cabin is there. It's where I go and paint. But I don't do it well."

"To paint or draw at all," she said, "is better than my stick figures."

He dared not say what he thought. Although svelte, her figure was by no means a stick.

Fortunately, she interrupted his thoughts. "Could we go to the university? I'd like to see where you teach. And maybe pick up a brochure."

Something sparked inside him. "Are you thinking of staying in the area?"

SEVEN

Christine tried to sound playful. "You think I should?"

His response was noncommittal. "Why not? Tens of thousands of tourists visit these mountains each year. It's a favorite place for Floridians to have a summer home. Many retirees choose to live out their golden years here. You could earn your master's in English at the university. But it's locked up over the weekend."

Was he just stating facts, or would he like for her to stay? If he could just like her enough, so that he wouldn't hate her when he knew her identity, then—"Matthew," she said quickly, "what kind of music do you like?"

They spent the next couple of hours listening to some of his CDs. She took off her shoes and sank into his comfortable couch with her legs drawn up against the seat. They both liked some of all kinds of music, from country to classical. They both knew the latest in popular contemporary Christian music. While some of the music played, they went upstairs to his loft and discussed his supply of books on the shelves. He preferred mysteries; she had a penchant for romance.

♋   ♋   ♋

Matthew hardly knew what he was saying on the way back to Mountain View. Strange how a supposedly intelligent man, a university professor, could talk trivia while his emotions ran wild and his mind hardly functioned. But he talked about the places they passed, the significance and history of various spots.

What to do next?

Ask her out?

From the moment they'd met, something inside him had changed. He seemed to have known her forever. Yet in another way, he knew her not at all, but he wanted to.

After returning to Mountain View, he parked his car beside hers next to the cottage.

Was she going to say good-bye? She turned toward him. That uncertainty about her surfaced.

"You've treated me several times this week, with free rafting, a couple of lunches at Slow Joe's, and lunch today. So, if you're game, I'd like to treat you." She glanced at

Mountain View's café. "Raimondo's has sandwiches, cappuccinos, and decadent desserts."

"How could I pass up an invitation like that?"

She looked delighted. "Go on and get us a seat, if you will," she said. "I'd like to check in with my grandparents."

Matthew had been to Raimondo's before. He waited outside the door, then watched when she hurried across the road from her cottage. She seemed eager to reach him; but when she began to talk about her grandparents, he felt her animation was because of them, not him.

"Want to sit out here?" she asked.

"First," he said, "there's something I want us to do."

He glanced around at the dimly lit room accented with Mediterranean decor, reminiscent of Tuscany, Italy. Christine followed as he ascended a few steps to the elevated section separated by a low wall. This, too, was filled with overstuffed furniture in rich patterns and textures.

Matthew gestured at a wooden-topped table that had inlaid checkerboard squares. "Okay, let's see what you're made of."

She sat in an easy chair, and he pulled up a straight one to use sitting opposite her. He made the first move with a checker. He won.

"No fair!" she scolded. "You went first. Cheater!"

"Okay, go!"

She did and won. "Two out of three," she said.

He let her go first, but he won anyway. "Ah." He leaned back. "Now we know who's the better man."

"That's a sick sense of humor," she blared. "And you only won by two little kings." She scoffed and shook her head. "Let's eat."

They went to the cappuccino bar and ordered.

He looked down at her. She tilted her chin and narrowed her eyes while a small grin played at the corners of her lips. "You think you're something, don't you?"

"Yeah." His eyebrows rose. "Didn't I just prove how good I am at checkers?"

Matthew loved their bantering, teasing, playing. But more serious questions lay in his mind. *What are you thinking, Christine?* he thought, as they ate their sandwiches and talked of trivia.

Did she think this setting romantic, with its aromas of food and honeysuckle and coffees and its fragrant piney breeze?

Did she like the intimacy of sitting at a small, wrought-iron table for two, reminiscent of an Italian outdoor café? Did she think there was significance to a man and woman, having eaten, to now sip cappuccinos—his a frozen vanilla, hers a steaming double mocha with a dash of whipped cream?

He had an artist's heart. Or maybe it was just a man's heart.

He wanted to paint the two of them together.

He couldn't.

Even more, he wanted to live it.

Could he?

Don't analyze, Matthew, just enjoy the moment.

He could appreciate the setting, the backdrop of high mountains, the lush foliage all around, the quaint cottages, the rhythmic coursing of water in a nearby creek, the call of birds, and the scamper of small forest animals. The flower boxes and beds in front of the café, the rustic fence, the deep blue sky brushed with streaks of gold and pink in the west, green plants, hollyhocks, tall golden yellow daisies with brown centers.

Most of all—a beautiful girl who had invited him here.

Payback—for his supposed kindness? Did she not want him to think she felt obligated?

Or, did she like him. . .in a special way?

Was she just a tourist passing through, passing time?

"I want to ask you something, Matthew," she said tentatively.

He nodded, feeling the taste of icy vanilla coffee on his tongue.

"Everything around here is so beautiful and interesting. I wonder. . . ." Her voice trailed off for a moment, and she ducked her head slightly as if shy, then gazed rather soulfully at him. "Do you know anyone who might be willing to give me a tour of the area?"

The sun slipped behind some of the high mountains. He glanced at the sky. Shadows threatened like trees divided. Limbs reached into the sky as if praying for the sunlight again. Shadows crept toward them. Where had the sun gone?

The day was dying.

Before he dared respond, Matthew rested his hands on his legs beneath the table, out of sight, as if he were just a man like any other and his deformity didn't exist.

The thought of her anywhere, with anyone, without him, tore at his heart.

After an eternal moment, he looked across at her like a man looks at a woman who has a soft, expectant glow in her gaze.

What a question she had asked.

Who, indeed, might he suggest to take his place?

EIGHT

"This is the Dam Road," Matthew said, stopping at an intersection.

Grinning at the surprise on her face, he said, "Look at the road sign."

She looked to her right. Sure enough, the sign read "Dam Road."

She glanced at him and grinned. "Things are not always as they seem, are they?"

He laughed, turned right, then drove into a parking lot. "And there's the dam. . . ."

He left the sentence dangling. She bobbed her head a couple of times as if to say, "What?"

"Fontana Dam," he said mischievously.

She gave him a mock-wicked look. "Are you trying to shock me?"

"What? Only yesterday we went to church. What

do you take me for?"

For better or worse paraded across her mind. However, she tried a wicked look again. "Wouldn't do to say." No, it wouldn't. She took him for so much more than she'd planned to find in her hero.

She took him for one of the most wonderful persons she'd ever known. He took time to show the area to her, a perfect stranger. Well, not perfect, just a stranger. He was a kind man. She had expected that, but she had expected him to be settled into a life typical of a thirty-year-old man—the wife, the kids, the job, the house, the car.

He didn't have those. He said he was content. And why not? He had his relationship with God. He had his dog, his jobs, his independence. But he'd lost so much. Even now, he strolled beside her with his hands in his pockets. He did not seem ashamed of them, maybe just aware that people stared.

They walked along the concrete and on top of the dam.

"Look out there," he said. "What do you see?"

Christine looked. "Blue-green water." The color of his eyes today. "Ripples? Um, let me try and be poetic. The slight breeze whips the water into ripples." She looked at him for approval.

He grimaced. "That's terrible."

She tried again. "Bordered on each side with myriad trees comparable only in China."

"You're learning," he said.

She gazed into the distance. "An island far out on the lake and a panoramic view of mountains in the distance."

He faced her and grinned. "Not bad for a westerner. Now, tell me what's beneath the water."

"Let's see," Christine mused. "I'd say underneath that water is lake bottom."

He burst out laughing.

She shoved him with her shoulder. "I mean, dirt. Or sand. Like river bottom. Bet it's not grass."

He lifted his eyebrows.

"Fish," she continued. "Or. . .an old boot."

"All that and more," he said. "There's a town down there." He looked serious.

"A town?"

"Yes. Houses, stores, roads, anything you'd find in a town. Also, there were copper mines with one hundred workers. The government stopped the mining, and the workers were told to vacate their homes."

"When was this?" Christine asked, interested.

"After the Japanese bombed Pearl Harbor in 1941."

"Was it necessary to put people out of their homes?"

He didn't know the answer for certain. A lot of the old-timers in the area still believed it hadn't been fair. "The government originally told them it was necessary to control flooding, improve navigation, and generate electricity.

All those things were true. But it was only after the war that people learned the dam generated power even before the project was completely finished. That power was used in the development of atomic energy across the mountains at Oak Ridge, and the knowledge gained there was used to develop the uranium for the atom bombs that helped us win the war."

She followed his gaze in looking out over the calm blue lake, the green wilderness, and the distant purple mountain majesties. She understood how the area got the name of "Great Smoky Mountains."

"This is the highest dam in the eastern United States," Matthew said.

"How high is it?" she asked, with an impish grin.

"Um." He hedged. "Close to five hundred feet, I think. I do know the lake is about thirty miles long. Let's go into the Visitors' Center. There's plenty of information there."

He opened the door for her to enter. She went over to a plaque and read it aloud. " 'The dam is 480 feet wide at its base. It holds back the twenty-nine-mile long, 10,640-acre Fontana Lake. Fontana Lake, created by the dam, has 240 miles of shoreline and an elevation of 1,727 feet.' "

Even more intriguing was the fact that six thousand workers came to build the dam. They built a large community with all kinds of stores and even a hospital. The project took about five years to complete.

She couldn't resist buying a couple of books and a video about the dam.

"Incidentally," Matthew said, as they walked outside again and past a man on a riding mower permeating the air with the fresh odor of new-mown grass, "a scene from the movie *The Fugitive* was filmed in this area."

"I didn't see that one."

"Have you seen the movie *Nell*?"

"Yes, Jodie Foster played the title role."

He nodded. "Her cabin is near here."

Christine recalled that the character Nell had grown to like the hero more and more. As Christine and Matthew related, perhaps she and Nell had something in common.

She liked Matthew.

Liked him?

Christine glanced over at the lake. To say she liked Matthew MacEwen would be like saying Fontana Lake, which could cover an entire town many times over, was a little trickle of water.

ৡ   ৡ   ৡ

On the way back from Fontana, Matthew didn't ask how long Christine planned to stay. Like a seasoned tour guide, he simply mentioned some of the area's points of interest. "Nearby is the Joyce Kilmer Memorial Forest."

"Oh," she said. "Joyce Kilmer is the poet who wrote

about only God being able to make a tree."

He nodded. "I'll get some brochures for you. But there are numerous places we can visit within an hour from here—Cherokee, Maggie Valley, Gatlinburg, Asheville—"

"Oh, look," she said suddenly, pointing to her right. "That sign says, 'Road to Nowhere.'" She looked at him quizzically. "What does that mean?"

"What it says," he replied, driving straight ahead. "It goes nowhere. It's a dead end, and nothing's there."

Christine looked back over her shoulder as if to see the phantom road.

"This is what I've heard," he explained. "While the dam was being built, people who'd been uprooted from their homes complained they had no way to get to their cemetery, particularly on Decoration Day, as many of them called Memorial Day. After much haggling, the government agreed to build a road to the cemetery. They started, but the road was never finished."

He pulled into the parking lot at the Information Center for brochures. His mind was partly on those and partly on the sign "Road to Nowhere."

Is that the road I'm on?

What was the speed limit for a heart that had been at an emotional standstill for years?

He'd already given himself warnings.

What would be the penalty for a runaway heart that broke the speed limit?

NINE

The following morning, Matthew waved a couple of tickets in front of Christine. "Today," he said, "we're taking a slow train ride on the Great Smoky Mountains Railway."

When he added that she might see Thomas the Tank, namesake of a children's TV show, because it was in town for a face washing, she clapped her hands, mimicking a child, and exclaimed, "Goodie, goodie!"

"We board in Dillsboro," Matthew explained on the drive to the nearby historic town, noted as being at the crossroads to the Great Smoky Mountains National Park and the Blue Ridge Parkway. "It's a two-and-one-half-hour round trip. We have an hour layover for lunch in Bryson City, then return."

He handed her a brochure. "When we come back, we can tour some of the houses, if you like. There are artisans, craftspeople, food vendors, musicians, all kinds of shops, even homemade fudge."

"Now you've said the magic word. Could we skip the trip and go for the fudge?" She laughed. He grinned, despite trying to look offended. She pulled her camera out of her bag. "Now, let's find someone to take our picture."

The nearby cars had the names of Cherokee, Piedmont, Fontana, and Silver Coach painted in bold colors on the sides.

"We'll be in Piedmont," Matthew told her. "You might want that as the background."

She struck up a conversation with an older woman who was delighted to take the picture. Soon, they boarded. "There're air-conditioned cars, coach, and open-air," he said. "I chose the air-conditioned."

"Couldn't you see more in the open-air?" she asked.

"Sure. More sunshine and flying insects."

She accepted that and sat next to the window, with him beside her. The engineer spoke over the intercom. "We're now embarking on our scenic journey across river gorges, through tunnels, over fertile valleys, and along the Tuckasegee River. You'll see the unspoiled beauty of western North Carolina in the spectacular Great Smoky Mountains."

Christine's hair moved softly around her face when she turned her head to look at Matthew with great excitement in her eyes. He saw the unspoiled beauty of the mountains daily. New to him was this unspoiled beauty from the West Coast.

He reminded himself to take a lesson from the train ride. *Savor the view. Enjoy the moment. Don't rush and chance derailment.*

The whistle blew, the chug-chug began, and the train moved slowly along the tracks. In the maintenance yard, Thomas the Tank Engine sat gleaming in the sunshine, displaying a freshly washed face.

When the engineer wasn't talking, Matthew added his own knowledge of places and events. "Those are the cars of the spectacular train wreck in *The Fugitive*. You can see pieces of the bus that the train ran into. This was the first time Hollywood ever used a full-sized train to stage a train wreck. They normally use model trains."

He pointed out a place where the river was very swift and kept washing away the bank. Eventually the people had piled old cars on the bank, most of them middle- to late-1950s automobiles. "They're now almost covered with kudzu vines."

They passed large tobacco, squash, and corn fields. "Every October," Matthew said, "there's a platform built in the center, then they cut mazes in the cornfield and people try to be first in getting to the platform."

"Why?" Christine asked.

Matthew shrugged and laughed. "An old ritual, I guess. But this I do know. Legend has it that many years ago the Indians found mounds of old turtle shells. So they named the river Tuckasegee, a Cherokee word for 'Turtle Town.'"

The engineer spoke over the intercom, telling them that as the train went around the upcoming curve, they could look around and see the back cars of the train and the caboose.

"I don't see it," Christine complained, looking out her window.

Matthew laughed. "You have to look to your right."

Holding onto the back of the seat in front of him, she sat on the edge of her seat and leaned forward. He watched her and savored the scent of a woman who smelled of freshly shampooed hair and a hint of lip gloss.

"Neat," she said, so close that he strained to feel her warm breath on his face.

"That reminds me," Matthew said. "Grandpa talked about prayer being like the rails for a train. The train is full of power and can run thousands of miles a day. But if there are no rails and it tries to move, it will sink into the ground. It can't go anywhere if the rails haven't been laid. He said prayer is the rail for God's work and His will."

She turned her smiling face toward him. "That's a great way to think of prayer. Have you painted prayer?"

Painted prayer?

The idea took his breath away. He could paint the wrecks, the wild growth, but could he do justice to the smooth rails? But then, if it was an analogy of prayer, the roughness might better depict human attempts to petition the Almighty. What an idea.

Their gazes held, suspended in eternity, hers questioning, his wondering. On a deep level, he wanted to try.

For himself, he wanted to paint her. But how to do either? How could he ever do justice to her clear brown eyes, smooth, silky skin brushed with a healthy glow, soft pink lips, delicate long lashes, a gaze that mirrored a lovely soul, fine hair that moved even with his breath when he talked. His hands wouldn't allow him to do what he wanted. His hands wouldn't allow him—

The voice sounded over the intercom. "We're heading into a pitch-black tunnel in a few moments."

Ah, he knew what red-blooded American males did in a situation like this with someone like Christine seated next to them. He clamped his hands together and willed them to stay that way. To offend her, to chance her revulsion, would be a hurt too hard to handle.

Then in the darkness, he felt fingers crawl up his arm and tickle his neck.

He yowled. "Unhand me, Woman!"

Others in the train laughed.

She had done what he dared not do.

He blinked at the bright sunlight when they came out of total darkness. Christine studied him thoughtfully. Was she thinking she would like him to be more aggressive?

"I was thinking," she said, "about your grandpa's thoughts on prayer. Like with the train, sometimes we can look back and see the results of our prayers. Right?"

"Exactly," he said with a wry smile. His hands had remained clasped during the entire tunnel ordeal.

෪   ෪   ෪

Over the following days, they toured all the places Matthew had previously mentioned, including the university, where he introduced her to a couple of teachers who taught summer classes. They visited the famous Biltmore House and Gardens in Asheville and drove up the parkway to Mount Mitchell, where they stood on a lookout with their heads in the clouds until a swift breeze brushed the clouds away. They looked out over mountain peaks displaying their lush glory for miles and miles.

"You're so blessed to live in a place like this," Christine reiterated after Matthew drove down the mountain a piece and stopped at the flowering Craggy Gardens.

"I know," he said. "I never tire of it. Even the same

view is different day by day."

When he took her back to her cottage, she asked, "Tomorrow, would you show me Catahoochee?"

"Cataloochee," he corrected, grateful for her mis-pronunciation. It gave him a moment to regain his equilib-rium. Should he take her to his most private hideaway—the place where he could go and pretend to be the great artist he was purported to have become?

Would it be wise? Didn't he need someplace where she wasn't?

Already, weren't his emotions like a raft caught on a wave?

Why raft? Not for the smooth water, but for the exhilaration of challenging the rough waters, the rapids, the falls. What would be the result? A smooth landing? Or going under the wave that came over, dousing him completely with icy water?

He could maneuver through almost any rapid and come out solid, land smoothly no matter how rough the rapid. But that was a physical challenge, and his hands were strong.

But wasn't the exhilaration always worth the ride? The smooth water had little appeal without the rapids and the falls.

So, maybe he'd land too hard and become completely doused by icy cold water.

Her question made him feel like he was on the Nantahala without a paddle and headed for the rapids.

Then again, she could go with him anywhere; and if it didn't matter, he would forget her. If she mattered, he would carry her in his heart and mind even if she were not physically present.

And Matthew didn't need to wonder if she mattered. She was in his heart and mind. He wanted to spend every minute with her. Never let her go. His hands ached to reach out and touch her, to feel her soft, smooth face, that delicate, almost translucent skin, those full pink lips, her dark hair that flowed with the slightest breeze, the long eyelashes that adorned her eyes that took his breath away. She seemed to trust, to care, to seek something from him.

But what?

What?

He didn't know. He just knew he wanted to reach out and take her hand and run with her. He wanted to know her. The words of a singer who plaintively wailed, "For your love, oh. . .I would do anything," touched the depths of his human longing.

I love her. I want her.

So much. . .so much.

Oh, God, what can I do? Pray that You take this cup from me?

You didn't take a more bitter cup from Your own Son.

89

Do I really want this taken from me? This feeling I have for this young woman? Or can I savor it? I don't want to dishonor her. Can I keep her in my heart and mind without dishonoring her? Let my thoughts and my wants not disrespect her?

Lord, I've accepted giving up the dreams I had for my life. Must I give this up, too? Yes, I know. If it isn't Your will, then it isn't best. But, Lord, I don't think like You. I think like a miserable, selfish, needy human being. That's what I am.

Yes, yes. I know. Your Word says I can do all things through Christ who gives me strength. Okay, I give it to You. I might as well. I'm not in control here. I can't make her love me in spite of my hands.

She had accepted the burned children on the rafts. But scars on a child are considered heartrending—not grotesque.

He had to find out. Would she, could she, tolerate his touch?

TEN

Boogerman Loop.

Rough Fork Trail.

Cataloochee Divide.

"Mercy," Christine exclaimed after hearing him rattle off such names. "How can you say those names so glibly? I bit my tongue just trying to say 'Nantahala Lake.'"

He laughed. "Gotta be a native. Those are some of the thirty-seven miles of trails through the Cataloochee Valley. Being a good tour guide, let me inform you that the Indians called this 'god-a-lu-chee.' In English, that's 'wave upon wave of mountains.' That's how it looks from higher peaks such as Moody Top."

"Oh," she groaned. "That must be terribly depressing."

He looked at her quickly, then saw her sideways mischievous glance. *Think hard, Matthew.*

"Okay, okay," he said. "So you made a funny. Moody—"

depressing. I'm a little slow today." He loved the way she looked at him triumphantly. "Moody Run is far from being low. In fact, it's a ski slope 5,400 feet high."

"Wow!" she said. "You ski?"

"Love it."

"I've never tried skiing." She could imagine his strong, lean frame on skies. He would be magnificent, taking the slopes with as much expertise as his hands expertly turned the steering wheel to make the curves or paddled a raft through rough water. "It sounds exciting."

"One way to find out," he said. "You going to stick around until winter?"

Only if you ask me. The words tripped across her brain. She mustn't put off any longer what had to be revealed. His reaction would determine if she could live the dream or awaken to the nightmare.

He continued his travelogue, enticing her with every word accompanied by the view of valleys and forests, wildflowers and streams. "Be on the lookout for elk."

"Elk? I would expect you to say bear."

"Well, those, too. Along with deer and wildcats." He grinned. "Don't worry. They're more concerned about encountering us than we are about them."

"I'm not afraid." She was with the man who would have given his life for her. She didn't doubt that he would do it now if needed.

"Elk used to roam these forests," he explained. "They're now being returned to this valley as an experiment to see if they can survive in what used to be their native land."

"You think we'll see them?"

Her eyes scanned the valley, then the forested mountains as they rode through what he said was one of the most remote places in the Great Smoky Mountains.

"They usually appear early morning or late evening. And, too, we're not as likely to see them near the road as we are from Grandpa's cabin."

Grandpa's cabin.

Is that when she would let him see, not an elk, but Christine Norwood for who she really was?

🦌   🦌   🦌

Matthew turned onto a one-lane dirt road, which he followed until he reached a little log cabin, hidden away in the thick forest. Beauty jumped out of the back and followed them inside, where the odor reminded Christine of an artist's studio with the smells of wood ashes and stale air mixed in.

Matthew left the door open and raised some windows that had no curtains. "I stand here sometimes and watch for elk," he said. "They're elusive. I catch a glimpse of one gliding gracefully through the forest. I want to look just one in the eye so I can paint it. Sometimes I go outside and paint the forest, hoping I will see an elk so I can include it in the picture."

Christine looked out but saw only trees.

"Come over here," Matthew invited. "I want to show you something."

She walked over to an easel at the corner of the stone fireplace. He removed a cover and showed her the unfinished picture of an old man.

"My grandpa," he said. "I come here and work on it periodically. I just can't capture him completely. There were so many facets to his character."

"I don't know a lot about painting," Christine confessed. "But I know this picture reminds me of you."

Matthew's quick glance and uplifted eyebrows, along with his saying, "I look ninety-three?" made her laugh.

"Not the age," she said.

Matthew folded his arms across his chest. "Okay, tell me."

"The eyes," she said, stepping closer to the painting. She put her hand up close to the portrait like a wedge along the nose, separating the two sides of the face. "The left eye looks kind and compassionate. The right eye looks like no-nonsense."

Matthew leaned away. "Are you calling me and my grandpa two-faced?"

"Isn't everybody?" she teased. Then added, "Except Elizabeth Taylor."

Christine loved the sound of laughter in his voice. "I've never heard that one."

"Sure," she said playfully. "That's how 'the great they'—whoever they are—judge beauty. If both sides of the face are the same or close to identical, 'they' say it makes a person handsome or beautiful. Elizabeth Taylor's face is the same on both sides."

Matthew frowned. "Now I'm afraid to look in the mirror."

She touched his arm. "Don't worry. Both sides of your face are nearly the same." Realizing she'd just called him handsome and beautiful, she lowered her hand to her side and focused on the painting.

Feeling awkward, she blurted out, "You want to paint me?"

He faced her then. All of him looked no-nonsense. "Yes. I want to paint you." His gaze was hypnotic. Sorrow tinged his expression and his voice. "You're too beautiful and delicate. There was a time when I could paint a blade of grass on which lay a drop of dew. A critic said it was so real he thought someone had spilled a drop of water on the painting."

Christine held her breath, looking at the sorrow in his eyes and in his voice. "I could paint an ant on a leaf and the onlooker would want to swipe that insect off the painting." He shook his head. "I can't do that anymore. My hands are strong, but they're no longer able to create that light touch."

He's telling me I'm too beautiful for him to paint. I complimented him. We're looking into each other's eyes, standing close enough to reach out and touch. Except. . . He had put his hands in his pockets. *He does like me. I know it. But he won't make a move, unless. . .*

Yes, this was the time. Christine knew that. It was time to talk about his hands and reveal her identity. He was open to that now. The opportunity might not ever come again. But still, she couldn't just blurt it out. "Do you. . .want to talk about it?"

"It?" he said distantly.

She swallowed hard. This wasn't easy. Why couldn't she talk about his hands as easily as she talked about his eyes and his face? She would try. "Do you want to talk about how you got burned?"

His face seemed as shadowed as the corner of the room. Then he stepped out of the shadows and walked to the window. A long, awkward moment passed. Finally he spoke. He gazed into the forest, a distant look on his face. "When or if we get to know each other better, then I'd like to tell you about it. But it's not something I talk about beyond saying that my hands were burned in a plane crash. Some of the memories of that day are just too painful."

His thoughts seemed to have gone off into another world—a world in which she wasn't welcome. Christine didn't press him. Maybe it would do him good to rant and rave about having lost a promising future. Or maybe he'd done that before, but it hadn't changed anything, so he didn't see the point of doing it again. Maybe he wasn't serious enough about her to want to confide. Maybe he was too bitter to be able to talk about it calmly.

And maybe she didn't want to hear that he had made the wrong choice in saving that girl instead of saving his hands—the means to his promising future.

No, she didn't want to say, "Thank you for saving my life." She didn't want to see his expression of rejection toward her that would reflect what he'd suffered when people looked at his hands.

No, she couldn't tell him now. Not at this moment. Maybe never. He hadn't minded showing her the painting of his grandpa. They had joked. Oh, she wanted to get back to that.

"Could I see more of your paintings?" she asked tentatively.

She saw the rise of his shoulders before he turned. "Sure," he said. He wore a smile, but he looked at the floor as he walked across the room. "They're in the bedroom closet. Many paintings were lost in that plane crash. Some were sent on to New York. I don't know where they are. My aunt and uncle may have gotten them. I didn't want them. They were part of my past. And for awhile I bemoaned the fact that I had no future. I was young and immature then." He shook his head. "I don't complain anymore. I have life and blessings."

Christine wondered if he felt that way or just wanted to. He didn't seem to be in pain, but she hurt for him.

He pulled out a canvas. "This one," he said, "was painted when I was a teenager in Korea. I titled it, of all things, 'Cherry Blossom Cross.'" He laughed lightly and shook his head as if that were foolish. "Look here, how the limbs form a cross of delicate blossoms."

"I see what you meant about your painting looking so real," she said.

"Yes. But no matter how real it might look, it's only a reasonable facsimile of the Master Creator." His hesitation and the ensuing silence made her wonder if he were as accepting as he seemed. He glanced at her and spoke thoughtfully. "I don't tell this to just anyone. But in the early days, I planned to paint a cross in every picture. When my talent caught the attention of major art critics, I renewed that dedication."

He pulled out another painting of crosses on Calvary's hill. It was beautiful, shining, like the gateway to heaven.

He put it on the bed, then laid another one beside it. He stared at the paintings. "My life is divided into before and after the plane crash. Before, for the world to see, I painted the cross in every picture because it's what I was doing for Him."

He drew a shaky breath. "Now, to be stowed away in this box, I paint the cross in every picture because of what He did for me."

Christine stared at the paintings. Her thoughts ran rampant.

Was Jesus' cross smooth? Shining? A beautiful picture of perfection like smooth marble? Or polished glass? Porcelain? Did anyone sand it? Did the Roman soldiers care if there were splinters or rough places? Did they care if worms and bugs were in it? Or sticky sap?

No! The beauty was in the person who died on that cross.

The cross was terrible. Therein lay the beauty.

She held her breath and stared unblinking at the paintings.

She wanted to tell Matthew that his rough-looking hands represented who he was, what he was. And therein lay the beauty.

She felt so choked, she couldn't speak.

In the silence, without looking at her, Matthew packed away his paintings.

ELEVEN

Christine stepped out on the porch, and Matthew pulled the door closed behind them.

"You didn't lock it, did you?" she said.

"No need. It's not likely anyone would come up here and take the furniture. Oh, it's comfortable and okay, but not the kind of thing anyone would steal."

"What about your paintings?"

He scoffed. "Believe me. If anyone cares enough about those paintings to steal them, they can have them. If a hiker or anyone needs to stop here, they're welcome."

"That's nice."

"It's not original with me." He pointed at a spot above the door. "See that sign?"

She stepped back and looked above the door at a wooden sign she hadn't noticed when they'd arrived. Pink and white dogwood blossoms bordered blue letters form-ing the word "Welcome."

"Grandpa put that up years ago, when hunting was still allowed in the area and this was his hunting lodge. He had the philosophy that strangers were welcome. He said that out here he was alone with nature but never lonely."

"Is that how you feel?"

"Sometimes." Matthew took a deep breath, his eyes looking ahead as if searching for an elk. Then he glanced back at her. "But I have my lonely moments." He smiled, then it faded. "Hey, don't go feeling sorry for me. I have a full life." He smiled that way of his that made her feel special. His tone of voice lowered. He spoke seriously. "I'm not lonely right now."

"Oh." She didn't want him to know how that lifted her spirits, how it increased her pulse. "Is that because you saw an elk when you stared at the trees?"

The thick growth of tree limbs blocked the sun, but a glimmer of light sparked his glance. "You got it."

$$\text{\textit{ø}} \qquad \text{\textit{ø}} \qquad \text{\textit{ø}}$$

The smile she gave him sent Matthew's pulses racing and sparked a flame in his heart. He thought he could read people rather accurately, and the page upon which he was looking seemed to convey positive messages. Surely she hadn't spent so much time with him just because he became a volunteer tour guide. They talked personally, exchanged likes and dislikes.

He hadn't wanted any particular girl before, but he wanted this one—in particular.

He'd been content; now he shuddered to think of life without Christine.

If.

If she could tolerate his touch, then. . .

Should he dare?

Nothing ventured, nothing gained. What could he lose? All the time men touch a woman's back or arm, meaning, "I'm right here; lean on me if needed." It was simply an acknowledgment that they were relating. That was all. Nothing unseemly implied. But he couldn't do it naturally like other men.

Nothing ventured. . .

We're at the edge of the porch.

You can do it.

If not. . .nothing gained.

What's to lose?

You can't lose what you don't have. If she can't abide your touch, you need to know. Now is the time. She's about to step on the first step. There are only two.

Slowly, deliberately, his hand moved toward her,

giving her time to know what he intended.

The blunt ends of his fingers tingled with anticipation.

He felt like he had when he was a child. His grandpa had put together an electric train, then said, "Now plug it in."

Plug it in? He'd been warned never to touch an electric socket. He'd been scared to death. But he trusted his grandpa, who looked at him with the same excitement young Matthew had felt. The train was going to go. It even had a smokestack. It had a whistle. He could hardly wait. But first he had to do the forbidden and plug it in.

His grandpa waited.

Matthew knelt in front of the socket, plug in hand so tight he thought he might squash it or else his fingers might break. He darted a glance up at his grandpa, who nodded encouragement. Slowly, slowly he guided the thing toward the wall. He held his breath and thought his heart was going to jump right out of his chest. Could his grandpa hear it?

Slowly, slowly he let the tip of the metal touch the socket.

Yiiiiii!

It sparked.

He let go of the plug and fell back.

He had been five years old and had been forced to

endure the awful humiliation of not being a man about it. He'd even cried because he wasn't hurt. No, the electricity hadn't shocked him. He was just a scaredy-cat. His grandpa ignored his tears and his humiliation and said, "Well, I should have showed you how to do this. I'm sorry. Just plug it in fast, like this."

His grandpa did it and survived.

"Now you try it."

Matthew had. They had laughed, then played with the train all day long.

He could survive this, too. He only hoped he wouldn't scream and fall backwards first.

Christine had to have seen it coming. Sure she did. That's why she shifted her position as she stepped onto the ground and exclaimed, "Oh!"

Matthew shoved his hands into his pockets. His fingers clinched like they were grasping that plug. He mustn't cry. She wasn't his grandpa. And he wasn't five years old.

She turned toward him. "I thought I saw an elk run past."

"They do that," he said, looking around for Beauty. He couldn't chance a whistle, lest it come out a sob. However, the dog came running, and Matthew threw in the dog biscuit. Yes, he still had his dog—man's best friend—who welcomed his touch.

He knew her moving away had been an unconscious move, denoting her inner revulsion. His hands anywhere on her body would be repulsive.

Her face flushed. He knew she hated her reaction. But she couldn't help it. He couldn't blame her. *You don't want a girl who isn't God's will for you.*

Do you?

He would get on his knees awhile before answering that one.

What did she think of him? She liked him. He knew they connected. But she'd failed the big test—being able to tolerate his touch.

She couldn't know how valuable these hands were to him after having lived for months without their use. They were one of his most prized possessions. He was thankful for what they could do.

But he knew what they couldn't do—and that was touch a woman.

Like Quasimodo, he could be respected, even loved; but he couldn't have the girl.

They'd already had the only train ride possible for them, but this time there was no end to the pitch-black tunnel.

Get over the "all or nothing" bit, Man. Don't wallow in self-pity.

Cherish what is. Don't pine away for the impossible.

Hadn't you already told yourself you were on the road to nowhere?

Count your blessings, Matthew.

You know, worse than not touching her would be. . . touching her.

TWELVE

Matthew talked until the tension drained away and he'd made himself accept his position as Number-One Tour Guide.

When he took Christine home, he reminded her that in a couple days, he'd be busy for two weeks. He had seven days to train ten people in kayaking on the Nantahala, after which he would take the group white-water rafting for seven days in Costa Rica.

He said as nonchalantly as he could, "Will you still be here when I get back?"

"I honestly don't know."

She looked troubled. She'd indicated she had a problem. He was supposed to be a friend. "Well," he said, speaking from his heart, "just in case, I'd like to take you out to eat tomorrow evening." He glanced at the sky. "Thunderstorms have been forecast, but I'd like to take you to the Jarrett House in Dillsboro."

"Oh, you pointed it out to me the day we took the train ride. And I've read about it in a brochure. That sounds great. I'll go shopping for a dress."

"It's a nice place. But like I said before, this is a tourist area; so as long as it's not a swimsuit, there's no particular dress code."

She laughed. "But it's a good excuse to go shopping."

§   §   §

Christine felt like this was a real date. Not like ones she'd had before, going to a movie or out to eat with a college guy. Not like the time spent with Matthew already. She had asked for that. But he had asked for this. She had a date with a man. And not just any man. This date was with the man she loved.

For years she had loved Matthew because of what he'd done for her.

Now she loved him for what he was and who he was.

Looking in the mirror, she approved the dress she'd found in a little shop in the nearby town of Sylva. The basic black dress had short sleeves and a rounded neckline trimmed with one row of silver sequins, and it fell to just above her knees. She fastened small silver earrings that had diamond centers. She thought she fit the description her grandmother often gave on dress code—tight enough to show you're a woman, conservative enough to show you're a lady.

The dress was inexpensive but, being a shoe person, Christine splurged on the black floral mesh pumps with the tapered toes and three-and-one-half-inch heels.

"Ready!" she said aloud, observing that anticipation colored her cheeks and put a sparkle in her eyes. She applied lip gloss. Already, she'd brushed her hair back into a twist and fastened it with a black barrette. Would Matthew think she looked pretty? And mature?

Matthew had said he'd come at seven. She thought the storm, now raging with full force, might delay him. He arrived five minutes early. She'd watched for him. When he parked at the side of her cottage, she ran out, wearing flats and holding two plastic grocery bags. One she held over her head and the other contained her camera and her new shoes.

"I was coming to the door," he said.

"I know you're a gentleman," she said, climbing in. "But I didn't want you to drown. I'm starving."

Halfway settled in the seat, she glanced at him, then took a second look. He wore gray trousers and a tailored, gray-and-white, small-checkered sport coat. The green silk tie against his white shirt deepened the color of his beautiful eyes.

"You look wonderful," she said.

"Thank you." He smiled. "Better close the door before you drown."

She did, while adding, "I've been all wet before."

"I remember," he said jovially, backing onto the road after she fastened her seat belt. He didn't comment on her looks. Well, maybe she'd failed in her attempt. Or maybe he wasn't interested in her—as a woman.

She assumed his relative silence was due to having to watch traffic closely in the blinding rain. She was aware of his nearness in the privacy of the car, with rain shutting them off from the rest of the world, the rhythmic sound of the windshield wipers, and the tantalizing scent of musky aftershave.

Was he as reluctant as she to think they wouldn't see each other for two weeks—maybe never?

After he parked at the side of the big white building, she asked him to put her camera in his coat pocket, then changed from her flats into the heels. Finished, she looked at him. He wore an amused smile while gazing toward her feet. He glanced up. "Oh, I should say I'm sorry to stare, but—" He did a mock clearing of his throat. "Great shoes."

The mischievous look in his eyes made her blush.

They hurried along the white wrought-iron railing across the porch, past the long window boxes full of multicolored impatiens, to stand beneath the canopy over the entry. Inside, the maitre d' led them to the reserved table-for-two near the windows across the front of the charming inn. While lightning crackled and thunder rumbled, Christine focused on the man across from her, the subdued glow of candlelight on the tables, the soft music in the background, and the quiet voices and soft laughter in the dining room set with fine china on white linen tablecloths.

She asked for the camera. "Let's ask the waiter to take our picture. But this is so special, Matthew, I could just cry. You'll have to tell me to say 'cheese.'"

"Maybe this will make you smile, Christine. Not that you haven't before, but you look totally gorgeous tonight." His voice was a whisper. "You take my breath away."

That took hers away. She was glad he hadn't said that sooner, as if reciprocating for her remark about his looking wonderful.

His gaze was mesmerizing, causing delicious little shivers to permeate her being. She could not look away. She thought the waiter deserved an extra tip for showing up at that moment with their menus.

"I've never tried catfish," she said.

"You must," he insisted. "A Southern delicacy. But. . ." He read from the menu. "So is the 'hand battered with the Jarrett House special recipe' deep-fried chicken. Ham's great, too, and the rainbow trout."

She groaned. "Catfish or chicken."

Matthew set the menu aside. "We'll get both, and whichever you like best is yours."

She closed her menu and gave him her best smile. "If you insist."

After the meal, they sipped cups of coffee and shared a piece of French silk pie.

When they finished, Matthew signaled the waiter for the check.

"Matthew, this has been the most wonderful evening I've ever had." The way he looked. . .at her. The special way in which they related. This had to be the moment to tell him who she was and why she came to the area. The timing seemed perfect. How to begin?

The tumultuous elements were going crazy outside. But that paled in comparison with the turmoil inside her. Maybe first she needed to let him know his hands didn't repulse her. She could not have gotten out of that plane. She couldn't have left her parents if Matthew hadn't taken her out. She had known they were dead. She hadn't wanted to know it.

Matthew's hand rested near the check holder that the waiter placed at the edge of the table. Christine moved her hand toward Matthew's.

ℒ   ℒ   ℒ

Matthew saw it coming.

He quickly picked up the check holder and opened it, looking at the numbers that didn't register. What registered was that he wanted neither Christine's pity nor her sympathy. Being a kind person, touching his hand would be a conscious move on her part, trying to make up for moving away when he'd reached toward her on the porch of the cabin. To make up for her revulsion, she chose to reach for his hand.

The situation reminded him of some of the reality shows on television. They tested the contestants by forcing them to eat a live bug, even though it repulsed them.

Eating a bug was a forced, planned thing. A person swallowed it with great difficulty, and some people couldn't even do that. Accomplishing that feat, however, didn't mean contestants would love to spend the rest of their lives eating bugs.

Christine's touch would prove what she wanted to feel, to be. . .not what she was.

She'd already proved that welcoming his touch was not a natural, normal, unconscious thing for her to do. She had to make a conscious effort.

For him, real acceptance had to be spontaneous, not premeditated.

Christine had courage.
She was trying to eat a bug, Matthew.
That's all.

THIRTEEN

The storm still raged on the way back to Mountain View. Both Matthew and Christine were relatively quiet. When he parked beside her cottage, Christine said, "It was a wonderful evening, Matthew."

"I agree," he said, "thanks to you." He squeezed the wheel and looked out at the electrical storm.

"You're welcome," she said.

What else could she say? Or do? She couldn't kiss him good-bye. She'd tried to touch his hand, intent upon telling him who she was, but he'd withdrawn. That had not been the time.

"I'll be in touch," she said.

He nodded.

Christine couldn't stand the silence, the tension, the confusion. He seemed so distant. "Bye, Matthew. I wish you well on your trip."

"Thanks." His glance darted toward her, then was again directed at the windshield.

She hadn't changed her shoes. She didn't care. Let them melt! What was a pair of shoes? "Don't get out." Judging from the way his hands clutched the steering wheel, she thought he had no intention of getting out.

Holding onto her plastic bags, she exited the car and shut the door. She didn't put the bag over her head. Looking into the darkness inside the car, she saw his silhouette. He still stared ahead. She was a few feet from her front door. At the door, she turned. She wanted to run back. Tell him everything.

But he began backing out onto the street. He'd waited. For what? For her to go inside to make sure she was safe?

From what?

Being struck by lightning?

She was struck by something more powerful than lightning. And the evidence was stinging her eyes and spilling over her cheeks.

She unlocked the door, turned the knob, reached in, and flipped the light switch on. She looked back and said aloud, "I love you. I love you," to red tail lights disappearing in the storm.

✢   ✢   ✢

All night long, the heavens cried and wind beat against the windowpanes. Christine wondered which was worse—the storm outside the cottage or the one inside her body, beating a sorrowful thud inside her chest and whipping her emotions to and fro. She felt like a tree had fallen on her chest and the branches had choked off any means of escape.

Her and Matthew's relationship started in the water. Now it had ended that way.

But this was water from within. It flooded her face and dampened her pillow.

Christine awoke from a fitful sleep to a cool, clean, crisp, and clear morning. The sun sparkled the yard, turning it into shiny Easter grass.

How could nature look so beautiful when she felt like such a failure?

She couldn't give him back the hands and ability he'd had before saving her life.

Apparently, there was nothing she could do for him. Nothing he wanted from her.

Slowly, a possibility began to tiptoe across her mind.

Later in the morning, she drove to the cabin in Cataloochee. He'd said the paintings didn't matter. They mattered to her. She selected three, then hurried to the car.

On the next available flight to New York, she scoffed inwardly. For one who vowed she'd never fly again, she was doing a lot of it.

She felt sure she was doing the right thing. She'd borrowed some paintings. Matthew couldn't possibly have a problem with that, could he?

$\mathscr{A}$ $\mathscr{A}$ $\mathscr{A}$

Matthew had returned late the night before. Two weeks had passed. Concentration while kayaking was necessary on the river. The trip had been great. For two weeks he'd been in control. His hands were skillful, admired for their strength. He'd conquered the river, the rapids, and the falls.

He wasn't on the river now, instead planted not-so-sure-footed on the slippery ground of human relations. Sitting on his deck, with his trusty dog at his feet, he lectured himself about reality.

He knew the impression given to those around him—the camp staff, guys at the center, workers at Slow Joe's, fellow church members, colleagues at the university, waiters and patrons at Jarrett House, and even strangers who passed them on their sightseeing adventures.

The impression was Matthew MacEwen's got a girl, and she's a knockout.

Lucky guy!

He'd noticed the look in their eyes as if they had a renewed respect for him. Hey, maybe Matthew isn't just the guy with the misshapen hands. Maybe there's more to him. Look at the girl he's with.

He didn't like how he'd look without her. Well, Matthew MacEwen had had his chance and blown it. He was like that old nursery rhyme. "Peter, Peter, pumpkin eater, had a wife and couldn't keep her." Matthew had no pumpkin shell and no chance of a wife.

But it no longer mattered how things looked.

Only how he felt.

Regardless, he had to go backwards with his life, to his life before Christine.

After a restless night, he called her cell phone number early in the morning. While it rang, he remembered the time difference if she were back in California.

She answered on the second ring, and the sound of her voice was not that of one who expected to hear from a telemarketer. More like someone expecting an important call.

"Hello," she said.

Matthew's heart raced like it did when he was going up on a wave or steering around the rocks in the rapids.

"How are you? Where are you?" He ran his questions together.

"I'm still here," she said.

He breathed a sigh of relief. He wanted her to be gone. He also wanted her never to leave.

"Matthew, I want to tell you something and show you something." She rephrased the first words he'd ever said to her after the crash. "I have something that belongs to you."

An hour later, with Beauty in the back, he picked Christine up in his truck.

"This can only be done at your cabin in Cataloochee," she insisted.

He couldn't imagine what made her so happy. But it felt wonderful relating to her on an easy level again. "Did you buy me an elk?"

"Oh," she said, laughing. "I wish I'd thought of that."

He laughed with her. "I don't think they're for sale." He couldn't imagine what she had in that thin, large box.

❧　❧　❧

At the cabin, Christine took the paintings out of the box and spread them on the couch.

"Those are mine," he said, looking at her curiously.

"I know. I borrowed them and took them to New York." She took a letter from her tote bag that she'd tossed on the couch. "You'll understand when you read this."

She watched him read it. She knew what it said. Bruce Canton had written it and shown it to her in New York. Bruce had shown the paintings to the art experts. They'd raved over the paintings and wanted more. They said his paintings were their greatest discovery in years.

Matthew read a sentence aloud. "These are a remarkable creation of a talented artist. Give us more."

The look on his face was not what she expected. His glance swept over the paintings, then back to her. "What's going on?"

"I took them to Bruce Canton. I wanted to do something. . .for you."

Why wasn't he pleased? Maybe it was just too unbelievable? Didn't he want this?

"You had no right," he blared.

Christine stammered with sounds that made no sense. Dying in the glare of his gaze, she finally managed to mumble, "I wanted to do something for you."

If he were angry about the paintings, what would he do when he knew about her? She'd been so wrong not to tell him right away. Her deception had backfired. She'd deceived him twice—once about the paintings and then about herself. No! Three times. She'd deceived him about her love for him.

He shook his head, closed his eyes against some kind of pain, then looked away. "I don't need that kind of help.

120

I never had fame, only some so-called experts' opinions that it could happen. I didn't really lose anything that I had. I'm not some charity case."

Christine slumped down on the edge of the couch. He turned from her with his hands in his pockets, speaking into the air. He couldn't even bear to look at her? She'd meant well.

"In that plane crash," he said, "more people died than survived. I don't know why my life was spared. But I do know I gained a dependence on God, an appreciation for life, a facing of my frailty and His omnipotence. I was doing fine—"

Until she came? Is that what he meant?

She spoke defensively. "Well, I was, too. And I don't see you as a charity case. How do you know the Lord didn't send me here to help you?"

He turned toward her then. He looked weary. "Christine, if the Lord sent you here to provide a way for my rough paintings to have meaning for others, then I will thank Him over and over." He confessed, "That's not really the source of my anger."

Christine stood. "Wh–what?"

He spoke low. "It's because you're making me miserable."

"You. . .you mean that?" She had failed. He didn't like her, and he would hate her if he knew she was the one who had ruined his life.

"Yes," he said, walking close to stand in front of her. "Please don't cry. The way you're making me miserable is that you've disrupted my calm existence. Now, everywhere I go, there you are. You are in my life, my thoughts, my dreams. But it mustn't be. I'm scarred, inside and out. You're beautiful and young and should not bother with me. I know you can't accept...all of me. You can buy yourself whatever world you want."

Christine stood, staring at him for a long moment, seeing the pleading in his eyes. He wanted her to leave. She could put an end to it once and for all. "I can tell you who I really am and how I came to have money."

He stared, his brow furrowed and his eyes full of questions.

Christine nodded. "I can make you even more miserable. You see, it is because of you that I have this money. It is because of you that I live. I couldn't tell you about it because I knew when I did, you would hate me. I wanted you to like me, even love me, before you knew."

"What?" he began, as if she were again speaking a foreign language. "Christine, your natural instinct was to recoil from my touch."

"It wasn't because of your hands. I can prove I don't feel that way." She had deliberately worn a tank top, low cut in back, just for this moment. She began to unbutton the shirt she'd worn over it.

Matthew drew in his breath, held out his hand to stop her, and stepped back. "Don't do this, Christine. Don't do something that will make us regret we ever met. I don't want to take advantage of you. . . ."

FOURTEEN

Christine's shirt slid down her jeans, onto the floor. Her generous curves, outlined by a tank top, stirred his senses.

He longed to take her in his arms, to forget all caution, to give in to his natural instincts, to shut out the laws of God. He wanted to love her, feel her in his arms, touch her, caress her, and let her memory haunt him forever.

Then her lips began to tremble, and her eyes flooded. He wanted to console her, tell her not to be embarrassed. But she turned from him.

He struggled for the next breath. "What happened to your back? Who did this? Oh, tell me. I'm so sorry." He stepped closer.

Her breath came quick then. She looked at him from over her shoulder. Her face was wet. "You're not. . . repulsed?"

"Repulsed?" He put his hands on her shoulders and turned her to face himself. "Yes, that you would be hurt so. But not. . ." He shook his head as if he couldn't believe she asked such a thing. "Not because you're scarred. I mean. . ." A short laugh, without humor, escaped his lips. "Look at me."

"We were scarred at the same time," she said. "You will hate me now. I'm the one who ruined your life, your career."

His brow furrowed. "What are you talking about?"

"I'm the girl whose life you saved on that plane seven years ago. The girl you carried from the burning plane. And because of that, your hands were crippled. I love your hands. You see, your scarred hands saved my life."

He blinked as if awakening from a deep sleep. "I thought. . .you'd died." He moved his hands from her shoulders and stepped back, as if seeing her for the first time.

Christine knew it. He couldn't bear to touch her now. She wanted to run away. She took a few steps toward the door but stopped in front of the window. Now that the words had started, she mustn't stop them. But she couldn't face him as she spoke.

"I was only sixteen, but I loved you for saving my life. You could have left me there and ran. All the news media said so. But you didn't."

She shook her head, looking at the forest beyond the window.

"Christine," he said softly. "That is the most beautiful sight I've ever seen."

She glanced over her shoulder. "Don't make fun of me, please. You have every right to hate me for ruining your career."

"I don't blame you."

"I know you don't directly. But saving me changed your life. You couldn't even talk about it."

"No, you don't understand." He came to stand beside her. "I was changed for the better. The painful part was because I thought you'd died. All these years I have thought I didn't react quickly enough. Or perhaps I added to your injuries when I picked you up. But you would have burned to death if I hadn't. I had to try." He shook his head as if trying to clear it. "I never saw your name in the reports."

Christine swiped at her wet cheeks. "My grandparents were responsible for that. They said I'd gone through enough by losing my parents and being in the hospital for a long time and that I didn't need the media hounding me. Their wishes were respected."

He nodded. So she hadn't been trying to seduce him. He felt ashamed for having misunderstood her actions. "Christine, you mentioned the possibility of God sending you here for a reason."

She nodded. "I thought He wanted me to thank you and to help you if you had a need."

"I do have a need," he said, again putting his hands on her shoulders and turning her to face him. "I need you. I love you."

⌇⌇⌇   ⌇⌇⌇   ⌇⌇⌇

Feeling Beauty against the calf of his leg, Matthew said, "Stay."

"Yes," Christine whispered.

She moved his hands from her shoulders and placed them against her cheeks, then turned her face to kiss each finger and the palms of his hands. Her love was healing his wounds.

Not even attempting to repress the tears flooding his face, Matthew cradled her face, her shoulders, her back, with his hands. His love was healing her wounds. His scarred hands were inviting her to be his bride, to accept his love, to become a part of his life.

Christine moved her head for a moment and blinked at the moisture in her eyes. "Oh, look," she said. "There's an elk, standing still, looking this way. At the edge of the forest."

"No," Matthew said. "Right now, I don't need to see

an elk. I don't need a river or a palette of paint. I only need to touch you, to hold you, to love you. You take my breath away, and at the same time you give me reason for breath."

"I know the feeling," she whispered, lifting her face to his.

Their lips touching, with one breath between them, they clung to each other.

And as he held Christine close, Matthew knew he had all that he wanted at the moment and for the rest of their lives. Only God could have brought so much good to them from such a horrible accident. And only God could have brought them together again after years of separation.

Joy filled Matthew's soul. A promising future lay ahead of them with their lives resting in His Hands.